FALLING with
KIERA
ELENOR POUNTAIN

Enjoy your read ♡
Elenor Pountain x .

Publisher: Elenor Pountain
Photocredit: Deposit Photos
Cover Design, Editor, Formatter: Maria Vickers

Content Warnings

Detailed sexual scenes and some detailed and implied abuse may trigger some readers.

BLURB

Kiera is young, beautiful and has her heart set on finding what her best friend has. Love. After too long on dating apps, she bumps into a good-looking guy at the pub. Little did she know, their comfortable friendship would become something all-consuming.

Ed has a dark past that has turned him into the man he is today, someone who needs control. When he becomes friends with a beautiful girl, her lightness brings him out from the dark. His past confronts him head-on, but will it jeopardise the future he didn't envisage?

Ed shows Kiera a side of her she didn't know was there. Kiera shows Ed there is a light to each dark side.

TAGLINE

Dating apps did nothing for your love life, and you wondered what was missing. You didn't realise all you needed was to be taken over his knee.

Contents

Dedication

To my readers, my characters come to life in your imagination.

FALLING WITH KIERA

Chapter One

KIERA

"So, this was nice. Thank you for dinner." I rush down to the tube station so that quickly he doesn't get a chance to respond. Why can't I enjoy a date? I roll my eyes at myself whilst standing on the platform waiting for my train.

I've been on the dating scene for what feels like forever, but there's always something wrong. I'm not asking for a lot, just someone who doesn't give off Ted Bundy vibes or someone who knows how to shower.

Last month, it was Jamie, whose teeth were so stained I couldn't work out whether he just had an unhealthy diet or bad hygiene. Either way, when he leaned in for a kiss, I felt like I could have passed out from the toxic fumes coming from his mouth.

A week later, there was Zach. Zach was hot and had a vision for his future. Unfortunately, that future was protein shakes and a gym bunny girlfriend. I like my takeaways and avoid the gym at all costs.

Two weeks ago, it was Mark, who was over the top with his touching and slobbering, and I practically ran out of the bar before my drink hit the table.

A week ago, it was Callum. He didn't talk the entire time we sat at the restaurant for our date. I got either nods in response to my questions or complete blank stares to complicated questions such as "What do you do for work?"

The tube rolls to my stop, and I hop out and head home, feeling a little depressed. As I walk, I can feel a warm breeze in my hair and decide to take a detour to my corner shop to buy some chocolate to brighten my evening cup of tea in my PJ's.

As I walk through my front door, I think about tonight. Jake is everything I thought I wanted. Confident, has his own place, enjoys his job and has the deepest brown eyes that I could lose myself in forever. Turns out, he isn't looking for anything other than a heavy petting session. He doesn't like to think about his future; instead, he thinks of the now and what he can have before he "has to" settle down. To him, settling down is a punishment for getting older. I don't want to rush into settling down, having a farmhouse full of kids or anything either; however, not needing to go on dates that make me want to drown myself in chocolate every week would be nice!

I sit in my PJs with a cup of tea, my chocolate and my phone, which has the dating app glaring at me with new notifications. More matches and messages. Ignoring the app, I call my mum. I need to hear her voice when I'm feeling…I don't even know what I'm feeling at the minute.

After seven agonising rings, Mum finally picks up. "Sweetie, how are you?"

"Hey, Mum. I'm okay. Just wanted to hear your voice."

"Another bad date?"

I laugh and fill her in on my latest failed attempt at dating. I don't know what it is about hearing her voice through the phone, but I can feel her warmth surrounding me like an invisible hug. I've not had the best run of dates. My mum talks about meeting people the traditional way instead of using an app. While you can answer a lot of questions, you don't experience that gut feeling.

Listening to Mum has made me realise that's what has been wrong. I've been talking to some of these people before going on a date with them, but I've not had any gut feelings. Whereas, if you meet someone in a bar, you can know if there's a connection or not.

I finish on the phone with my mum and pull up the dating app, my finger hovering over it. Deleted.

JESS SITS ACROSS FROM ME IN SHOCK. WE'VE COME OUT for a drink and catch up. I am telling her about a guy I met in a bar. The sex was great, but there were some serious red flags, like his constant texting.

As we sit and catch up, something feels off about her. She is on edge and keeps looking around.

"For someone who's on cloud nine, you have one hell of a frown on your face. What's up?" I ask.

"I'm not sure. I feel uneasy, and I have no idea why. We're having a lovely time, and I'm in a really good place mentally. I'm not sure what this feeling is. You ever get the feeling that someone is watching you?"

Jess looks around again and still seems a little spooked. I scan the crowd at the restaurant and can't see anything or anyone out of the ordinary. I feel for her, but I can't sense anything that's off, so I say gently, "Maybe it's because you're in a good place and you're expecting something to go wrong? But it won't. You're smashing life right now."

With my words, she acts a little more at ease with herself, but I can tell she's still on alert. I try to distract her as we carry on talking. Somehow, time leaps ahead, and it's last orders. I swear, when we're together, we enter a different time dimension. It only feels like an hour has passed, but it's been quite a few. We finish our meals and drinks, then head out, both needing a decent night's sleep.

After our goodbyes, I begin to walk down the road towards the tube station but stop suddenly. I don't know what happened first: the gut-wrenching scream that I realize is Jess or the gasps and crash of a bottle. I spin around and shout for Jess, but she is already on the ground. I quickly run to her side; someone has already called for an ambulance and the police. One of the people in the crowd fills me in on what happened. A blonde attacked Jess. The bottle is on the ground, so we ensure no one else goes near it.

Within minutes, the ambulance and police arrive, and the police take my statement so I can ride in the ambulance with Jess once the paramedics confirm she is okay to move. I call Gavin from Jess's phone to let him know what is going on and where we are going.

I'm sitting in the waiting room, waiting for Jess to be assessed. My mind is circling, and I don't understand why anyone would attack her. She's literally the kindest person I know. She wouldn't hurt a fly. I spoke with Gavin on the phone—first time speaking to her boyfriend, and it's to tell him she was attacked—he should be here soon.

The door swings open, and in struts this handsome man with a walk of authority and his back straight, making a beeline for me. Going on what Jess told me about Gavin, this has to be him. My girl bagged herself not just a hottie but someone completely devoted to her.

Once Gavin checks with the police and nurses about Jess, we introduce ourselves properly. He then goes into Jess's room while I leave to freshen up and grab us some decent coffee.

Chapter Two

KIERA

It's been two months since Jess' attack. We've spoken every day, and I'm heading round to their house tonight for dinner. Gavin is going to wife her up anytime; I can feel it in my waters.

I'm waiting for a cab with the fanciest bottle of wine I could buy. Well, not really. It was £20, which I think is a lot for a bottle of wine. When I'm in the cab, it hits me. I want what Jess and Gavin have. I know I wanted it someday, but what they have is beautiful. Mutual respect, huge attraction to one another—and not just looks. He loves her goofy side and every part of her like she does him.

I arrive at their home and head up to the penthouse. It's stunning, especially compared to my small flat, and yet daunting at the same time. I've not been in someone's house that's this rich before. Within minutes, those daunting feelings melt away. Yes, Gavin is wealthy, but he is just a person. We laugh, drink, eat and chat about utter nonsense.

Tonight has made me more determined to find what they have. Love.

After Gavin moves into his office to take a phone call, Jess turns to me. "Come on, Kiera, what's up? You've looked a little down tonight."

"I'm just feeling a little fed up. I want someone to share my life with, but going on dates with morons is really getting me down."

"Take a break from dating. It's draining, especially when there's no connection. Have some time to yourself, think about what you want your future to look like, and who knows, someone may just bump into you."

I smile at Jess' words. She's right. I need to concentrate on my vision for the future, and it'll happen when it does. There's no point in forcing it with the wrong person or people.

I get home a little after eleven and decide to make a list of what I want in my future.

- Easy and comfortable relationship.
- Someone who loves me unconditionally.
- Passion.
- Love and lust.
- Spontaneity.
- Reliability.
- House with a garden.
- Kids.
- Growing old together, but happily, not going through the motions.

Satisfied and feeling a little better, I climb into bed. I text Jess before I drop off.

> Me: Thank you for tonight, love you xxx

A WEEK HAS GONE IN A FLASH, DURING WHICH WORK has been hectic. I don't think I've eaten a decent meal since I went to Jess', and I'm exhausted. But I'm heading out with work friends tonight to get a release. We have been working hard on an account we're hoping to get. Marketing is a tough business to be in, but it's one I love. It's fast-paced, ruthless and full of passion.

I meet Jake and Sarah at the local pub. They are on the same team as me but are working on different projects. Drinks soon flow, and I feel the stress leaving my body. Also, judging by the electricity between them, I assume there is something going on or about to happen between Jake and Sarah. The more we drink, the more the sparks fly. I am a little jealous when I catch Jake staring at Sarah whilst she's laughing. His expression softens as he watches her, and I also see the lust in his eyes as his gaze roams over her face and down her body. It's as if he is committing every inch of her to memory. As she laughs like a hyena, which never fails to be infectious, he stares at her lips like he wants to devour them.

I leave them to it and dash to the toilets. I feel the

warm fuzziness of the wine taking over, which is strangely comforting. Whilst in the ladies, I hear two girls giggling about a fit guy at the bar. He sounds intriguing from what I've heard so far. Apparently, he's tall with brown hair and green eyes. They are discussing the fact that he is apparently on a date he looks bored with. Sober Kiera says I need to head back to Jake and Sarah, and tipsy Kiera wants to go to the bar and check him out. Let's see who wins!

As I leave the toilets, I spot Jake sweeping a stray lock of hair from Sarah's face and see her blush a little. Those two are definitely going to get together. I'm so distracted by the love story unravelling before me that I don't notice the man in front of me until I walk into him. I mumble my apologies, wondering if it's the wine making me feel tingly when I glance up at him.

Oh. My. God. I mean, Gavin is beyond handsome, but this fine specimen standing in front of me is divine! He's only a few inches taller than me, making him around five nine maybe, and he has a masculine frame that his suit perches on perfectly. When I see his stubbled face and those green eyes, I wonder if it is the guy the drunk girls were giggling about.

"I'm so sorry," I say again, unable to tear my eyes from his.

"Don't worry about it, love," he says casually as he steps past me to the gents. There's something captivating about him.

Straightening myself out, I head back to Jake and Sarah, who appear deep in debate about something. It is a turn of style compared to the moment I witnessed moments ago.

"… and if you wanted to reach the right demo-graphic, you wouldn't add a bloomin' pop song to it!" Sarah said assertively to Jake.

"Just because it's the older generation we want to reach doesn't mean they don't enjoy a pop song!"

"Guys, what's going on?" I'm confused. Their words sound fierce, but the energy field around them could power the whole city.

"WE'RE JUST HAVING A MINOR DISAGREEMENT ON which song choice to use on the new rise and recline chair account we've won," explains Sarah.

"What do you think, Kiera? Do you think a pop song would grab the attention of the demographic we're trying to reach, or should we be like every other company and use a slow, soft speaking voice?" Jake counters.

"Why wouldn't it work? It could also reach those who care for older people rather than just ignoring the advert. Just a thought. Anyway, I'm heading to the bar. Another round?" After small nods from both, I leave them pondering my opinion.

It's nearing ten, and the bar is still busy, which is great. Thursday is the new Friday in London, after all. I'm trying to catch the attention of the barman when my view is blocked by the green-eyed man.

"Fancy bumping into you again." He grins. When I see his smile, my knees become slightly weak. His teeth are a brilliant white, surrounded by perfectly shaped lips, and a brown beard that has a few speckles of grey to match his hair. His eyes are light but have a darker edge around the iris.

"I am sorry about earlier. I was distracted," I explain.

"Ed." He reaches for my hand.

"Kiera." As I take his hand, I notice they are smooth with a couple of calluses, but he has a nice, strong grip. There's a tingling sensation. What is that? The wine?

I release him when the barman finally comes my way. I order a round of drinks, say my goodbyes and head back to my friends, who seem to be in a much better mood than when I left them. They must have sorted their little disagreement because they are back to sweetly glancing at each other when the other isn't looking.

We stay for another half hour before saying our goodnights. They live in the same area, so they head off on the tube together. I'm in the opposite direction and walk with earphones in and tunes on as I make my way to my platform.

I'm in my own little world when I hop on the tube. Enjoying my music and looking around the carriage, I sense someone watching me. Many have their heads down, reading whatever is on their phone screens, whilst others are nodding off to the gentle sway of the train.

I calmly turn my head to check out the rest of the carriage, and there he is. Ed. Smiling and sitting with one ankle on his knee, he looks completely relaxed. He gets up and comes to sit in the empty seat next to me.

"Hi again." He flashes those pearly whites at me.

"Seems to be a habit of yours, bumping into me." I smile back at him, knowing full well I hadn't been paying attention to where I was going earlier.

Ed laughs lightly, which makes my stomach flutter. What is this?

We idly chat on our journey until I stand up, ready for my stop, and Ed stands, too. "It's either a coincidence you're getting off at the next stop, or you're going to kill me in a dark alley," I say, laughing, but a small part of me is a little wary.

He laughs so loud it makes everyone look at us. "It's a coincidence, love." As the train pulls to a stop, he hops off and walks up the endless steps with me.

Chapter Three

ED

Alex set me up tonight good and proper. "Go on this blind date," he said. "You won't regret it," he said. If it wasn't for how my night ended up, I might have murdered him tomorrow. Zara was lovely to look at, but she had nothing of interest to say. I honestly don't care that her new favourite designer is now using vegan leather, which she finds utterly appalling. She spoke constantly for what felt like hours, not taking a breath until I escaped to the gents. That was when I bumped into the most beautiful human I'd ever seen in my life.

The bump literally sent electric shocks through me. The woman had soulful brown eyes and brown curls that fell around her shoulders. I quickly scanned her body and licked my lips, thinking about all the devious things I could do to those gorgeous curves. I snapped my eyes back up to hers. I could get lost in those brown pools for hours, and I silently cursed my bladder when it alerted me that I needed to actually use the gents. She straightened herself and walked away from me whilst apologising again.

I headed back to the bar and my awful date only to delightfully find her snogging some other poor guy. That was a lucky break! As I moved to the open space at the bar, I found the woman I'd bumped into. She swayed a little, drawing my attention to her perfect ass. Obviously, this was fate, and I had to speak to her again.

And that is why I'm walking out of the tube station with the most beautiful woman in the world. I have no intention of sleeping with her tonight. She has a vibe about her, and honestly, I just want to make sure she gets home safely. Kiera made a joke earlier about killing her in a dark alley, so to assure her, we take a well-lit route to ease any concerns she may have.

"I find it fascinating that on the same night that I could have had the worst date ever, I met a beautiful and interesting woman," I say, trying to be smooth, but I hear myself nearly tripping over the words.

"Well, from what I heard in the ladies, your date wasn't going to end well, and you may have had a few women lining up to take you home tonight." She sounds amused.

"Wait, I was being spoken about in the toilets? Why?" I chuckle, not quite believing it.

"You're an attractive man who very clearly didn't want to be on that date tonight." Kiera looks at me, smiling.

I stop walking for a second because she takes my breath away.

"You alright?" she asks, appearing concerned.

I grin and continue strolling. We've already passed my apartment, but I don't want her walking home late on her own.

As we round the corner, I see four flat complexes. "This is me," she says with a small smile. I have a feeling she doesn't want to walk to the one she lives in whilst I'm here, which makes complete sense—stranger danger and all. "Thank you for walking with me, Ed. It was nice to meet you." Kiera stretches up to kiss me on the cheek, and as much as I want to kiss her properly, I don't want to make her feel unsafe.

"See you around, Kiera." I saunter back towards my place, looking over my shoulder to see she has gone. I really hope I do see her around.

Six A.M., and my alarm clock blares at me. I drag my ass out of bed to get ready for a jog. I do the same route every morning, but today, I want to switch it up and maybe jog past Kiera's complex. Not in a stalker way, but I do want to see her again. It does sound like a stalker thing to do, though.

I'm chastising myself whilst jogging in that direction, and when I stop to have a drink, I see her. The sun is hitting her hair, giving it a beautiful glow. She's reading something on her phone whilst, I'm assuming, listening to music with how her head is bopping.

She looks up and sees me staring. Now, I feel like a definite stalker. *Crap, she's heading over. I stink!*

"So, not going to kill me in a dark alley but not past a bit of stalking?" She laughs, thankfully.

"I change my route up every week. Can't believe I haven't seen you about before," I lie.

"Well, if you're tired of running, fancy walking with me?" Kiera's eyes are sparkling this morning.

Delighted, I escort her to the station, figuring the extra steps will count instead of the jog I intended. We chat whilst going along the road. She asks where I live, so I point out my building as we pass.

"You walked past your house last night to walk me home?"

How do I respond without sounding creepy? "Yes, but I wanted to make sure you got home safe."

She smiles, and we stroll the short distance to the station, talking about whatever comes to mind. We reach the station all too soon, but I wave her off and jog back home, thinking about a beautiful brunette who seems to be smart, funny, and easy to be around.

I step out of the shower and dress for work, trying to focus on what I need to do for the day, but all I can think about is potentially running into Kiera again. This is maddening. I should be thinking about the analysis I need to finish because we have our annual accounts review coming up, but I keep wondering what she does for fun. I've only had a couple of conversations with her, and I want to get to know her more. She is comfortable to be around, and I honestly enjoy her company. Taking a deep breath, I force myself to finish getting ready and head to the station with headphones in whilst going through my to-do list for the day.

It's now eight in the evening, and I'm finally on the way home to enjoy a bite to eat, a shower and an early night. As I'm trudging to my flat after a long, mentally draining day at work, I appreciate the night sky. It's a deep purple, with the clouds lined with pink.

In front of me, I see a silhouette I recognise. She looks like she's slouching rather than the straight, self-assured posture I've witnessed over the last couple of days. I walk towards Kiera, pausing my music as I near her.

"Hey, stranger," I say as I get closer.

"Oh…hi." She's sniffling and wiping tears from her cheek. Even in the low light, her eyes look swollen.

"Kiera, are you okay?" I put my hand on her shoulder, and she freezes. Realising I've made her uncomfortable, I quickly pull back.

"Just a bad day." She's shaking me off.

I know from a friend that you can either push to see what's going on, and a woman will appreciate the support and caring, or you can give them space, and they will tell you if and when they are ready. It's a fine line. So, I'm going with the safest option. "I'm here if you want to talk. Would you like some company on the way home?" I receive an answering nod, and we walk in a comfortable silence, past my home and towards hers.

"Thank you for walking with me," Kiera finally manages.

"You're welcome. Are you going to be okay?"

"I will be. Just a tough day at work, and then someone didn't like hearing the word no, so he gave me a load of abuse." Her voice is quiet, and I can barely hear her.

"I'm sorry about work. Is it looking to turn around soon? And why did you have to say no to someone?" I want to cuddle her and tell her everything is going to be alright, but instead, we keep walking.

"Work will get there. It was a bad project day. The no..." She stares down at the ground as we move. "The no is a guy at work. New guy who thinks that he is God's gift to women. He doesn't like the word no, and he, and I quote, 'never gets turned down.' I must be a quote, 'frigid bitch with major mental issues if I don't want a piece of him,' and that was the politest thing he said."

My anger levels rise. How dare anyone have the audacity to say that to another person. I don't know Kiera that well, but she seems to be a genuinely nice person. The fact someone has treated her like this rattles me. "Kiera, I'm so sorry someone has treated you like that. He will have his comeuppance. Jerks like that will say what they want, and with any hope, he'll say it to the wrong person and get his ass kicked." That gets a small smile out of her.

"Have you eaten?" she asks, sounding a little brighter. I shake my head. "Fancy sharing a pizza? I'm in the mood for junk food." She grins. It's infectious, and I can't help but grin back with a chuckle.

"Absolutely." We make our way to hers. Kiera is walking a bit taller now.

Chapter Four

KIERA

We order pizza and sit on my sofa, chatting like we've known each other for years when, in reality, it's been a few hours total dotted over a short period of time here and there. We talk about our work, families and personal lives like it's been a lifetime friendship. I've not had a male friend who's so easy to be around and doesn't immediately make a move. It's nice to just be with Ed.

Our pizza arrives, and I don't think twice before diving in. Some women are conscious about eating in front of other people. I am not those women. I love my food and hate the gym. Luckily, I have a fast metabolism. Ed is also chomping through his pizza in a messy fashion, which I find oddly attractive in a man.

"What?" Ed chuckles.

I feel like I've been watching him eat for too long. "Nothing, I just admire anyone who can eat like I do." I smile back at him.

We demolish the pizza and wash it down with a glass of wine. It's only then I glance at the clock and notice it's eleven o'clock. How did it get so late? Ed sees me looking at the time.

"I best get home. Got an early start tomorrow. I hope you're feeling better, and thank you for the pizza. Next time, it's on me." He smiles as he stands to leave.

"Oh, don't be daft. I'm not going to lie; I would have eaten the whole thing, so you technically saved me there." I'm laughing, but I would happily eat another half a pizza right now.

Ed leaves, and I head to the bathroom to wash up before bed. I feel much better than I did on my way home from work. I brush my hair and climb into bed.

It's been a good week since I ran into Ed, and I'm missing the interaction with him. Work has been much better. I voiced my opinion and told the new guy that he had no right to talk to me the way he did. He actually apologised. As I'm walking out of the coffee shop with my five-shot dose of happiness before work, I notice a familiar figure sitting outside with his laptop.

"Hey, stranger," I say as I walk over.

He looks up. His eyebrows are creased together with a confused expression on his face that changes into a wide smile when he sees me. "Fancy seeing you here." Ed gestures to the seat next to him.

I glance at my watch; I have ten minutes to chat

before I have to head to the office. "So, what's with the face before I sat down?"

"Oh, just some emails. It's really hard not to respond with 'seriously, how dumb are you?'" He laughs, and I laugh with him, completely understanding where he is coming from.

Before I know it, my time is up, and I must leave. We say our goodbyes, and I head off.

"Hey, Kiera!" Ed shouts before I can move too far from the table. "Here's my number. Text me later, and we can have a drink after work if you're free?" I smile and promise I'll text him before leaving him.

As I sit at my desk, scrolling through my emails and checking my to-do list for the day, I feel a flutter in my stomach when I think about Ed giving me his number. I eat my breakfast bar in order to calm the fluttering— it must be hunger.

My morning flies by, lunchtime is approaching, and I've got a hankering for the local deli's sandwich of the month: teriyaki beef on tomato bread with onion mayo. My mouth waters thinking about it. When I can get out of the door, I'm bee-lining for my food as my stomach growls at me, and as I wait for it to be prepared, I text Ed.

> Me: Finish at 6 tonight, let me know where you fancy that drink.

When my sandwich is in my hands, I walk over to the flower beds. People like to sit on the wall around them and eat lunch. It's nicer than eating at your desk.

I sit and dig in, and I don't hear my phone ping until I've nearly finished devouring my sandwich like a starved woman.

> Ed: Great, meet you at the bar where you ran into me lol.

I smile at his text, thinking about the feeling of electricity when we bumped into each other and saunter back to work, stopping by the coffee van on my way. I have three meetings this afternoon, and they require a lot of caffeine to get through. My first meeting goes by smoothly and without a hitch. The second, however, starts a headache. This one is amongst other teams in my company. One of the other managers is stomping her little feet because she isn't getting her own way. Luckily, my manager is in there fighting in my team's corner. The other manager wants the high-income account for her team, but the fact remains that we are the team that won the account. Before the third meeting begins, I take a quick break and step outside for some sun and fresh air. I check my phone to see a message from Ed.

> Ed: Change of plans, meet me at the Italian restaurant on the corner near the bar. Booked a table for 18:30

I smile; he knows I like my food. I return to the office feeling better and looking forward to dinner later. The third meeting is, thankfully, nice and easy. I catch up on my emails before leaving for the day and heading to the Italian restaurant to meet Ed.

As I'm walking, my phone rings. I grin when I see Jess' name on my screen. "Hey, you!" I exclaim. It's been a week or so since we last caught up, and I miss her.

"Hey! I miss you. Fancy a weekend away? Jet included?"

"My God, YES! Text me the details. I'm just heading to dinner with a friend."

I hang up, feeling excited about whatever she has planned. I love that woman fiercely.

Chapter Five

ED

Kiera has been on my mind for days. Seeing her this morning validates all of the feelings I have about wanting to spend more time with her. When she texts me about drinks, I wonder if she will find time to eat today. I know she's busy with work at the moment. I call the local Italian restaurant and book us a table before quickly firing a text to her with the details. I'm sure she'll appreciate the food whilst we catch up.

As the end of the day edges closer, I start feeling nervous. She didn't respond to my change of plans, but she's read it. Hopefully, she has simply been too busy to text back. I stroll down to the restaurant and hope she comes. Why am I nervous? This isn't a date. I am just hanging out with a new friend.

I sit at our table and realise I'm not sure what she likes to drink. I know she drinks wine, so I play it safe and order a bottle of white. As I check my emails, I feel a light around me. *That's odd*, I think. Then I hear her say my name. Is she the source of the light? I smile at her and ask if she'd like a glass of wine to save me from drinking the bottle by myself. She laughs and accepts the offer.

We talk about our days. Hers has been better, thankfully, and the new guy who was incredibly rude to her has been avoiding her at all costs. I am happy she has not been the brunt of any more abuse from him. I told her about my week so far and that I have an easy couple of weeks ahead now that the annual accounts are over, which is a nice reprieve. After we order our food, I hear her stomach grumble.

"Have you not eaten today?" I ask concerned.

"I have. I devoured a sandwich at lunch. No idea why I'm so hungry." She shrugs.

I smile. It's a nice change to see a woman with a huge appetite. I know a lot of women who have had the ability to eat like a horse, but they are too self-conscious to eat in front of others, especially men. It has always baffled me, but then, I am not afraid to admit I have no idea what goes on in a woman's mind. I'm thankful Kiera feels comfortable around me.

A waiter brings over our food. Kiera ordered a carbonara with extra garlic bread, and I got classic lasagne. I eat here most weeks when I am working late and have tried most of their menu, but I particularly enjoy the lasagne. The minute Kiera puts a bite of food in her mouth, she makes a little noise. I glance up to see her close her eyes as a hum escapes her. She looks happy. I take the opportunity to study her face. I've not looked at her this intensely before. Her brown curly hair frames her face beautifully, her skin is unblemished and appears smooth to the touch, and she has the slightest hint of freckles on her nose. They are cute.

She opens her eyes and notices me staring. "What?" she says, still chewing her pasta.

It is at that moment that I feel the light take hold, and I burst out laughing. "I appreciate a woman who loves her food," I simply say. She rolls her eyes and carries on eating.

I haven't felt this light in years. My past always made me feel a little darker than others around me, although you never really know the demons people are fighting. I feel comfortable with her and enjoy the warmth she brings to me. I push the darkness to one side and enjoy this time.

We finish our meal, and when she pops to the ladies, I pay. I have a feeling she'd put up a fight if she was at the table. She's walking back and gets her purse out of her bag when she sees the black folder with the receipt on the table.

"It's taken care of." I smile.

"No, that's not right. Let me pay half."

"Nope, my treat. I'm more stubborn than you know." I grin, happily winning.

Kiera huffs at me, her cute frown disappearing. Raising an eyebrow, she smirks and says, "Well, if this is the game, Mr, at least I know how to play it next time." She winks when she says next time, and I get a little flutter in my stomach.

We're on the tube home, chatting like we've been in each other's lives for years as the gentle sway of the train lulls Keira to sleep. When she finally dozes, her head falls on my shoulder. Not the first time this has happened to me on the tube, but at least this time, she's not a complete stranger.

My shoulder feels warm, like she's a ray of sunshine heating my cold body after a long time in the darkness. I haven't felt this for years. Yes, I've dated, but nobody has made me want to spend more time with them. It's more than her personality; it's her whole person.

Our stop is coming up, and I gently wake her. "Kiera, we're up next."

She opens those blue eyes, and my breath catches. I can search her soul and know I will find nothing but light and happiness. She smiles and stretches before standing up. When we leave the station, she's quiet, but I offer to walk her home, and she doesn't object.

"You okay?" I ask.

"Hmm. Just sleepy."

I suspect there's more to it, but we stroll in comfortable silence.

"Thanks for dinner, Ed. I had a nice time." Her mouth curves into a sweet smile that melts me.

I have the sudden urge to kiss her, but instead, I say, "You're welcome. Catch up later in the week?"

After we say our goodnights, I head home,

wondering what on earth is going through my head. She's a sweet girl, and we get on well. She doesn't need to be kissed by someone like me, though. I walk through the door and head straight for a shower before bed.

Chapter Six

KIERA

After Ed goes home, I enter my flat feeling a little deflated. I have no idea why because we had such a wonderful evening chatting, laughing and enjoying each other's company. Before he said good-night, I swear it looked like he was about to lean in and kiss me, but he didn't. Is that why I feel this way? Pushing away my thoughts, I strip and get into a hot shower. The tube was warm and made me sleepy. Now, I just want to get into bed and feel snug and fresh.

After three hours of tossing and turning, unable to fall asleep when I'm so tired, I reach for my phone. I fire a quick text to Jess to see how she's doing, check my emails and scroll through social media. I find myself searching for Ed even though I don't know his surname. I can always use his number to see if he's on one of the platforms if he's used it to sign up, of course. *Is that stalkerish?* I laugh to myself and continue.

I find his profile and look through it. Most of his

information is hidden because we're not connected, but I scan through his public pictures. I find one of him with people who I'm assuming are his family. He has a look on his face that I have not seen yet. It's dark and a little dangerous, and it makes me curious because everyone else has smiles plastered on their faces. I carry on scrolling and find more of him with that expression. His green eyes seem like they're coming out of my phone and staring straight into my soul. There's something behind them that's intriguing. Then I make the rookie stalker mistake and accidentally like his picture. That was taken 4 years ago. *Agghhh!* I try to unlike it, but the social media platform hates me and isn't doing what I want it to.

I throw my arm over my face in dismay, then hear my phone ping. It's two in the morning, which means Jess isn't replying to me. I see his name and feel my cheeks burning.

> Ed: Stalk much?

Shit, shit, shit! I text him back with no idea about what I want to say.

> Me: Well, professional stalkers wouldn't have made that rookie mistake. But yes, I was being nosey. Lol.

> Ed: You should learn from the master. I checked out your profile last week.

Me: Find anything interesting?

Ed: Many things

Me: Like what?

Ed: What did you find, other than a picture of me looking miserable?

Me: Many pictures of you looking miserable. Lol

Ed: I liked the picture of you in the peach dress. It makes your eyes stand out.

My blush creeps up from my chest to my cheeks as my heartbeat notches up slightly. I love that dress and have received many compliments when I wore it to a work's night out.

Me: Thank you. Why are you awake?

Ed: Couldn't sleep. You?

Me: Same. What's on your mind?

Ed: A girl.

Me: Oh, do tell! I love a bit of gossip.

I say that, but I feel a small pang of sadness. We have not known each other long enough to want to date, but I like him. He makes me feel safe and equal. Most of the guys I date make me feel vile like I'm only good for one thing, but I shove those thoughts away because I still sleep with them. I'd love to know how many women actually orgasm during sex. So far, my success rate is zero. I sort myself out when they leave.

I'm waiting for the three dots to finish. He's either typing an essay or he's distracted.

> **Ed:** She's pretty. Well, more than pretty. Gorgeous. But she doesn't play on it. She makes me smile, laugh and feel a little lighter when I'm with her. I don't see her often. Nothing has happened between us, but I'd like to see where it goes.

> **Me:** See how it goes. If you develop stronger feelings, make a move. She'd be a fool to pass you up.

> **Ed:** Ha-ha! Thanks for the pep talk, love! Go to sleep.

> **Me:** Night

I put my phone back on the charger and try to sleep. My mind is racing. I'd love to know what kind of woman he finds attractive, how she makes him laugh, and what he meant by making him feel lighter. As I'm drifting off to sleep, I see a notification pop up. It's a friend request from Edward Green. I laugh and doze off.

IT'S BEEN A WEEK SINCE THE STALKING INCIDENT. EVEN though I haven't seen Ed because our schedules have been crazy, we text most days. I actually have a date tonight—set up by a friend at work, so I'm not confident. I mean, we're friends, but I wouldn't say we are close enough for her to pick my life partner. But we'll see. Ed has been asking what the guy I'm going out with is like, and I tell him the truth: I have no idea. It's a blind date; however, I tell him that we're going to the Italian restaurant he took me to last week. I loved the food there.

Work keeps me busy all day, but thankfully, I brought my favourite dress to change into. When I shut down my station, I take my dress into the toilets at work to change before I touch up my makeup and take a selfie. I send it to Ed.

> Me: What do you think? Will I do?

> Ed: You look beautiful.

> Me: Thanks.

I leave the office feeling confident. I've kept my makeup light and am wearing the peach dress that is flattering. I plan on eating my body weight in pasta.

On my stroll to the restaurant, I feel a little nervous. What if I don't get on with him? I don't know anything about him other than his name. I don't even know what he looks like.

I take a seat at our table alone and wait, ordering a

glass of wine to settle my nerves. Whilst I'm people-watching, a man comes to the table.

"Kiera?" he asks. He's got dark blond hair that is short on the sides and slightly longer on top, which has been gelled into position. His hazel eyes go straight to my boobs. Cracking start if he can't look at my face first!

"Hi. Yes, that's me. Are you Sean?" I smile politely, standing to shake his hand.

"Yep, that's the one," he says curtly, sitting opposite me.

The waitress takes our order shortly after he arrives, and I'm shocked that he orders for me without asking what I want. "I'll take the steak with chips and a side salad. Well done. She'll take the tuna orzo salad. Peroni for me and water for her."

The waitress looks at me but walks off without saying anything. I just stare at him. First, he murdered a perfectly good steak by having it well done, and second, how dare he order for me! I can feel my anger rising, but as I open my mouth to tell him he is out of line, he starts talking about himself. Leaving no gaps to butt in. I down my wine in seconds. This is not going well.

When the waitress comes back with our food, she has a small smile on her face when she places a carbonara in front of me with another glass of white wine. I glance up at her in shock. How did she know? How was he going to take it? I tucked in, not giving a shit about his thoughts. I love my pasta, and no man is going to come between me and that longstanding relationship.

"Excuse me. You've brought her the wrong dish. Not that she can send it back as she's already eating it," he said angrily, cutting his steak.

"Sorry, sir. The order was changed before I took the request to the kitchen. I've also been asked to tell you to never order for a woman you don't know." She winks at me and walks away.

Sean is muttering to himself, clearly in shock that someone has dared to go against him, and takes a bite of his poor steak. Still chewing, he talks, and food spits out of his mouth. "You should watch that pretty little figure of yours instead of eating enough pasta to win a man versus food competition."

I slam my fork down. That's it. No one gets to shame me or treat me this way.

"First of all, Sean, if you had even bothered to ask me what I wanted for dinner, you'd know that I like pasta. Secondly, you do not get to tell me what I should and should not eat. I can't believe I've been put on a date with someone like you!" I'm angry, and my back is straight and tense, which has forced my boobs out. Of course, he's staring at those whilst I seethe. Before I can finish my wine, I feel someone behind me. Assuming it's a waiter or waitress, I angrily shove food in my face.

"Well, Kiera, I used to be a personal trainer, so I know how to look after your body—"

Sean is interrupted by a voice I recognise, but I have never heard this tone before. His voice is deeper and has a rough edge. "Before you finish that sentence,

I suggest you either get up and leave before she floors you or finish your dinner alone. Kiera…"

I look up to find Ed grabbing my bag and wine and gesturing for me to follow him. I smile at Sean and leave without another word.

Ed says something to the lovely waitress who brought me pasta instead of salad. I can't hear them, but she winks at me as she walks over to Sean's table.

As I'm about to ask Ed something, I hear Sean shout. When I turn round, I can't help but laugh. The waitress has "accidentally" spilt his second beer over him. He's starting to really shout at her when the head chef comes out of the kitchen. I've never met the man who has made my stomach so happy, but my God, he's a mountain. Sean takes one look at him and walks out of the restaurant. I turn back to Ed, who is eating his lasagne with a smirk on his face and a twinkle in his eye.

"So, you changed my order?" I ask, finishing my pasta, wishing I had some garlic bread. As if by magic, the lovely waitress brings some over. I'm moving in here. Who do I have to marry to make that work?

"When you said you were coming here for your date, I found it a coincidence that I was here after work for dinner tonight." He winks.

"My guardian angel with a voice deeper than a demon, it seems." I chuckle.

"We all have demons, Kiera. I'm just friends with mine now."

As I giggle and eat my bread, the man mountain comes out of the kitchen again.

"Signora, I apologise you had to sit with that awful man. His card has been charged with your meal this evening and a bottle of wine to take home. As compensation, of course." He winks at me.

"Oh, you didn't have to do that. I would have happily paid for the meal. Especially as your lovely staff are so deliberately clumsy." I smile.

He waves off my suggestion and reaches for my hand. "I am Marco. You, my bello lady, I believe are Kiera." I stare at Ed, who is still smirking. I know he comes here a lot, but I didn't realise he is close to the chef. I smile at Marco as he talks to Ed in Italian, who, to my surprise, replies fluently.

I lean back in my chair, drink my wine and watch the interaction with huge interest. I take in the Goliath chef, Marco. He is handsome. He must be at least six feet tall with a bald head and a black goatee that has speckles of grey running through it. Through his chef whites, I can see muscular arms. His hands are the size of a table, and as I look at his hands, I can see a wedding band that I assume lions can jump through whilst it is on fire. Of course, he's married. No woman in her right mind would turn down a handsome man who can cook. My attention refocuses on Ed. His mousy brown hair had a slight curl to it with some stray greys coming through. It is styled messily and is very sexy. His green eyes are filled with humour as he speaks to Marco in Italian. His mouth moves in a way that makes me stare at his lips and wonder what they'd feel like to kiss.

Marco waves and heads back to the kitchen, and

Ed turns to me, his lips curving up into a devilish smile as he crosses his arms. I quickly snap out of my daydream.

"Enjoying the show?" He winks and finishes his food.

I blush whilst the waitress from earlier comes over. I notice she speaks to me first but is friendly with Ed. She looks like she is in her forties with a trim figure, curly dark brown hair and kind brown eyes. As she reaches to refill my wine, I see a wedding ring. She reaches out towards me when she is done.

"Maria. I'm Marco's wife," she says, smiling. Of course, that makes sense. How is she so trim?

"Lovely to meet you, Maria. Thank you for helping me tonight."

"Marco and I see many dates in here, but that man deserves every bit of karma he gets." She winks and walks off.

"You know the restaurant well then?" I question Ed.

"I've known Marco and Maria since they opened this place. I love Italian food, and when I tried Marco's lasagne, there was nowhere else I wanted to go. We've formed a wonderful friendship, and I've helped them out when they needed a cash injection." Ed sounds so nonchalant, and it makes me very curious about his background.

"You have shares in the business?" I really am nosey.

"And as much lasagne as I can eat." He grins.

Once we finish our meal, Maria brings me my togo bottle of wine, making me smile, and we leave for the station. I feel Ed's hand on my lower back as we head down the steps to the platform. I don't tense when he touches me; instead, it makes me tingle. Must be the wine talking.

On the platform, he leans down to whisper in my ear, his lips slightly brushing my ear, making all the hairs on my body stand at attention. "You look phenomenal in that dress. Sean doesn't know what he's missing." Before I can respond, our train pulls up, and we step on, finding there are no seats, standing room only. The train is loud, so conversation is out of the question unless we want to shout.

Rounding a sharp turn, I lose my balance and fall into his chest. I look up, and he has a smug smile on his face. I quickly readjust and blush. The train feels like it's racing tonight. It could be the wine, or it could be that I normally find a seat, but it does feel like it's going faster than usual. I find myself staring at Ed's chest. He felt hard underneath his shirt, which makes me want to touch him more. I quickly look away before he catches me gawking at him.

We've spent time together before, but I've never felt this pull to him. I think it's because he saved me tonight from that horrendous date. When I glance up at Ed again, he's studying me. His eyes appear to be a shade darker than they were at Marco's.

Our stop comes up, and we jump off the train and head up the stairs to the street.

Chapter Seven

ED

I have never been as angry as I was earlier in the restaurant. When Kiera told me she was going on a blind date, I had to make sure it went well. I won't admit this to her, but I'm glad it didn't. This jerk shows up, doesn't compliment her on how beautiful she is, and then proceeds to treat her like an object throughout their date.

I was already at Marco's when she entered. I'd finished my afternoon work in there so she wouldn't think I was spying on her. The memory of her walking in, her dress hugging her figure and flowing around her, her hair down, curling over her shoulders...she was an absolute vision. Marco took one look at me and grinned when he saw my reaction.

"She's the one you're really here for. I thought it was my food!" He grinned.

"I can't explain it. She's a light that I need to be

near like a bloody moth." I suddenly felt ashamed that I was stalking my new friend.

"Darkness and light belong together, *amico*." He returned to the kitchen.

Maria clocked my reaction, too, and smiled. She's been trying to find me a woman for years, but she doesn't know my past or my dark side. Maria and Marco are wonderful friends and understood the assignment when Kiera's date began immediately acting like a dick.

I pull myself out of my head and watch Kiera walk up the steps to the station entrance. Even in that floaty dress, her ass looks fine. I have an overwhelming urge to hold her, kiss her, make her mine. But I get myself under control and jog up the remaining steps to be by her side. We take our normal route home, and as we walk, we laugh about her date. I tingle when I hear her laugh. It's almost as if she makes the dark clouds part to make room for her sunshine.

We're crossing the road when she trips. I grab her before she hits the ground, and she is laughing so loud I can't help but laugh with her. "Are you okay, Kiera?"

She stands up and wobbles slightly. I think she's hurt her ankle because she's leaning on her other leg. "Yeah, one of my special moves that. Tripping over nothing and rolling my ankle." She holds onto me as we get to the other side of the road.

"You've really hurt yourself. Come up to mine, and I'll put an ice pack on it."

"Don't be silly. I've got peas at home." She backs

down when I stare at her. I don't want her limping home in pain. We are literally outside my apartment.

She holds her hands up in submission, making me smile on the inside. I wonder what else she'll submit to. I help her up to my apartment. Unfortunately, the lift is out of order; therefore, I sweep her into my arms bridal style to carry her up the stairs. This makes her squeal and giggle. There's more of that sunshine that I'm loving lately.

"I'm not broken, just slightly sore. I can walk, Ed," she says.

I adjust her slightly in my arms so I can swat her ass whilst we're on the last few steps. "You'll do as you're told." I wink and notice her breath catch as her cheeks turn a shade darker than the wine has already coloured them.

When we're inside, I set her down on the countertop in my kitchen and grab my first aid kit from the bathroom. As a runner, I've rolled my ankle a lot, so I have learnt how to make it better. Returning to her, I can see Kiera leaning back on the countertop, looking around. Her back is arched, and I picture myself pulling her hips towards me, making her scream with pleasure. I shake my head and chuckle. I have to stop, but then again, it's just in my head—a little fantasy doesn't hurt. She hears me and snaps up. I am disappointed she's no longer in position, but it does mean I can see her face now.

"Having a good nose, were we?" I smile, setting the kit on the counter next to her, and she blushes. "I'll give you a tour once I've strapped you up." I can't help but smirk at her when I say that, mostly because I want to see her reaction. Her eyes widen slightly, and she bites her bottom lip. It's going to take every ounce of control not to kiss her.

I gently pull her leg towards me, remove her sandal and rub the already swollen ankle. Kiera lets out a little moan. I'm considering strapping myself up to regain my control. I take out the icepack and place it on her ankle, holding it in place.

She gasps. "Oh, that's cold. And before you say it, I know it's an ice pack." She smirks.

The corners of my mouth turn up in an honest smile, not initially realising I'm rubbing circles around her calf with my thumb. Kiera is breathing a little heavier. I want to think it's because I'm making her feel something, but it might be because the wine is wearing off, and she's in a lot of pain.

"Drink?" I ask, suddenly remembering I haven't offered her one. She simply nods her head. "Hold this." I point to the ice pack whilst grabbing the wine and two glasses. Once poured, I turn back around to see a single tear rolling down her cheek. Is she in pain? Is wine the best option?

I put the glasses down beside her and wipe away the tear with my thumb. She leans into my touch. "Are you okay? Do you need anything stronger than wine to take the pain away?"

I see a flash of a smile before she's back with me. "I'm alright. Just can't believe I'm so stupid and tripped over nothing. Nothing hurts like hell!" She laughs.

I take over, holding the ice pack, moving it round to the back of her ankle, which makes her arch her back a little. "Does it hurt anywhere else?"

She shakes her head, not breaking eye contact. I hand her a glass of wine, still staring into those gorgeous blue eyes. I want nothing more than to slide my hand up her leg, make her moan and forget the pain.

I'm lost in my thoughts for a moment, feeling a stirring in my trousers when she breaks the silence, "You look very deep in thought there, Ed. Care to share?"

I may have been imagining it, but I swear she put more emphasis on the word deep. It appears I may get myself into trouble with this one. I grin and move the ice pack round to the front of her ankle, making her gasp again.

After a few more minutes, I remove the ice pack and rub her ankle. She bites her lip. *Control, Ed. She doesn't need darkness.* Then I remember what Mario said to me in the restaurant, "Darkness and light belong together, *amico.*"

I rub some tiger balm into her skin before strapping her ankle with a support bandage. Letting her leg slide down slowly, I reach for my own glass of wine next to hers. "You'll need to rest that ankle. No running, gym or tripping over nothing for a while."

She laughs so loud I swear my kitchen brightens. "Oh, Ed, how I value your humour." Kiera hops down off the counter, clearly forgetting she's just been bandaged up and stumbles. I catch her by wrapping my arm around her waist and dragging her closer to me. I can feel the tension and electricity between us. I brush a stray curl from her face and tuck it behind her ear.

Fuck it.

I grab the back of her neck and pull her towards me. Her lips are soft. I move my mouth against hers, and she kisses me back. That's when I lose control. I push her against the counter and kiss her with more passion, and her hands dive into my hair. My arm is still around her waist, supporting her. I move my hand down to grab her ass and swiftly lift her back onto the counter, and her breath catches. My hands grip her hips like she's a lifeline in a stormy ocean.

I break the kiss, moving my head back slightly to search her eyes. Kiera is breathing as heavily as I am. I've not felt a kiss like that before. It is like we are fire and ice. Pure chemistry. Her eyes stare into mine, and before I can think, I'm back on her lips, biting the bottom one like I've wanted to do all night. She moans into my mouth. I slide her off the counter, carrying her to the sofa, our kiss unbreakable. Laying her down, I'm on top of her, between her legs, fully aroused and pressing myself against her. I manage to push both of her hands above her head and hold them there with one of mine whilst my other roams down the side of her body, squeezing her delicious thigh, which trembles under my fingers.

My brain kicks back into gear, control takes over, and I pull back.

Chapter Eight

KIERA

What the hell was that? It was as if my body and senses were on fire. Nothing mattered in that moment. I forgot the pain and just felt him. Passion like that is something you only read about; I never thought I would ever experience it.

But he stopped. He has a faraway look in his eyes, and his eyebrows are drawn into a frown. The way his lips are moving ever so slightly looks as if he's having a conversation with himself, and he's not happy. I don't want him to stop. The throbbing between my legs is excruciating, and I really don't want to have to sort it out myself. But watching him back away and move off of me, I know I'm going to have to.

"Hey…you okay?" I ask. I can barely hear my own voice. It's so quiet in here, and I don't want to shock him by speaking at a normal volume, but I didn't mean for it to come out as hushed as it did.

"I'm sorry, Kiera. I didn't want…didn't mean to…

I'm sorry." He doesn't look at me. This is my cue to leave. I stand up and remember my ankle as the pain shoots up my leg. *Shit!*

"Kiera, you need to rest your ankle. Stay for a bit until the swelling goes down some more. I'm sorry about earlier. I shouldn't have kissed you like that."

"Ed, look at me." He finally meets my gaze. I don't know what I'm seeing; there are so many emotions in his eyes. "It wasn't expected, but it was a great kiss. You certainly brightened up my evening." I laugh, which wins me a smile. He gets up and grabs my wine.

I stay at Ed's for a while longer until the wine is finished, and then I announce that I'm okay to hobble home. The gentleman he is, he insists on escorting me. More to ensure I don't put too much weight on my bad ankle or fall over. Walking to my flat with his arm around my waist, I still feel the same thick energy around us. I'm shamelessly leaning on him, hoping for another one of those kisses. He walks me up to my flat and says goodnight at the door. Such a gent. I am a little disappointed, but I don't want to lose the friendship we've built. It's easy, fun and reliable. I mean, the man showed up on a blind date to make sure I was okay. And, frankly, thank goodness he was there.

No sooner do I hobble to my bedroom than I hear a knock at the door. I have already taken my dress off, and the knock startles me. So naturally and clumsily, I fall over nothing. Again.

"Kiera, it's Ed. Are you okay?"

"Yeah, just me being me. Come in. I'll be out in a minute," I shout back, but within seconds, he's there helping me off the floor. I become very aware that I'm in only my underwear—a nice lacy black set, but still—and have only one sandal on.

"Um…I just wanted to say…" He is holding me; I can feel his grip tightening on my bare skin. I grab his head and pull him to me. I need to kiss him. I want to feel that fire burning again.

He picks me up and sits on my bed with me straddling him. He has one arm around my waist and the other in my curls. I'm still gripping his lush hair and his back. He is growing beneath me, and I gently rock against him, earning myself a low growl, which sends a shockwave of vibrations through me. I want more, so I bare down on him, swerving my hips a little more.

He stills me. "Kiera," he says, still kissing me. It almost sounds like a warning. I stop immediately. His tone is authoritative, but I can feel him smiling against my lips. Why am I so turned on right now?

I pull back to look at him, searching his eyes to try and gauge what he may be thinking and if this is going where I want it. Before I can speak, he stands and places me on the bed. "I have to go, but I'll text you later to see how you're doing. Please rest that ankle and work from home tomorrow." And with that, he leaves. I honestly don't know how I feel at the minute, but what I do know is I'm going to take some painkillers before I go to bed…after I lock my door.

I lie in bed and can't get comfortable. My ankle is sore no matter where I put it, but mostly, I am restless. Ed started something earlier that I desperately wanted him to finish. Thinking back to the kiss and how he made me feel, my skin begins to tingle.

I reach into my bedside drawer and grab my vibrator. I need a quick release; otherwise, I'm not going to sleep. Closing my eyes, I picture both moments in my head. Especially the time he said my name, his tone making it sound like a warning. I turn my toy on and start massaging myself down there, and I'm immediately stimulated. Normally, it takes a while, but he's really got me going. As I'm running through our kissing scene, my phone rings. I see his name. I answer, not removing my vibrator.

"Hey," I say, trying not to let on what I'm doing.

"Kiera, I just wanted to… What are you doing? It sounds like you're out of breath. Did you fall again?"

I giggle. "Just lying in bed." My voice sounds husky, and hearing him is spurring on the orgasm I desperately need.

"Oh, what are you thinking about?" His voice has changed. It's deeper, like when we were in the restaurant, and he told Sean to go and then said my name.

"That kiss."

"Well, here I am, thinking I was being a gent by leaving and not taking advantage of you. Maybe I should have strapped you up differently." Oh God, my mind is racing. I can't even reply, but a slight moan leaves my mouth, and he chuckles. "Stop now and unlock your door." He hangs up.

I'm so close, but something tells me to do as he says.

Minutes later, I'm back in bed. The painkillers I

took when I got home are helping the throbbing in my ankle but not the throbbing between my legs. I hear my front door open as I sit back down on my bed. He walks into my room, freshly showered and wearing shorts and a t-shirt. I can see the muscles in his legs and arms, and I lick my lips in reflex. I don't realise I am biting my lower lip until he saunters closer to me.

"Keep biting that lip and see where it gets you."

I grin but don't release it. He growls and lifts me further up the bed. I couldn't help but giggle. He's between my legs, raising one above his hip, his hand slowly stroking it from my ankle to my thigh, where he squeezes me.

He bends closer to my body and moves the hair from my neck with his hand, leaving my thigh a little cooler now that his touch isn't there. He presses his lips to that sweet, sensitive spot, and my hips automatically buck.

"Kiera…" Oh God, there's that tone again. I swear he's going to make me come just from saying my name like that. He bites down on my neck, his hands shifting to rub his fingers against the now-soaking spot between my legs. "Oh, Kiera, what a mess I left you in."

I moan a little too loudly as he touches my clit, circling it a few times before moving his fingers down to my entrance, plunging two fingers straight in. I'm not going to last long at all. He finds my G-spot instantly. I was starting to wonder if it actually existed. No man I've slept with has been able to find it. But Ed…he's pressing and teasing it like he knows my body better than I do. I come in seconds. I'm panting heavily like a dog in heat; he looks at me with a smug, devilish grin as he raises his fingers to his mouth and licks off my juices. I can't stop watching him. His green eyes seem darker. Everything about him seems darker, but I am enjoying the aftermath of my orgasm too much to care about anything else right now.

"So, you wanted to say something when you called me?" I ask lazily as I prop myself up on my elbows.

"I wanted to apologise for losing control with you, but it seems you didn't need an apology. Just an orgasm." He quirks his eyebrow at me.

"Why were you going to apologise for that? It was hot."

"I like to be in control, but you in that dress and then not in that dress made me lose control."

"Which is why you stopped." There's a story there I'm not going to press for…not right now anyway.

He opens his mouth, but I lean up and seal my lips against his. His electricity takes my pain away, and he's an amazing kisser.

"Kiera, I can't stop here. I want to do so many things to you." That's it. I kiss him again, hoping I let him know how much I want him. He growls into my mouth, his voice low when he says, "I warned you."

Tingles shoot up my body. Before I know it, he flips me over and holds my hands behind my back.

"Have you been tested recently?" he asks, breathlessly.

"Yes, I'm clear and I'm on birth control. You?" I cannot wait to feel him inside me.

"Yes, same."

My head is on my pillow as he drags my ass to him with his other hand. I hear him pull down his shorts, and then he thrusts into me. No warning. My endorphins are exploding with each powerful thrust. He's gripping my hip hard enough to bruise me. He pauses for a moment. I hear something, but I'm not sure what's happening because he's still holding me down. The next thing I know, my hands are being bound with something thin, and he's grabbing both of my hips, thrusting into me at a punishing rate.

I can't tell how many times I come, but I feel like I'm about to pass out. I have not experienced sex like this. I've also never been able to come during sex. My mind is swimming right now. He drags me up by my hair, which, surprisingly, doesn't hurt, pulling me backwards onto him as he leans back on his feet. I can feel his powerful thighs beneath mine as he lifts me up and pushes me down with such force I can pass out from the pleasure.

I lean my head back to kiss him. He stills momentarily to kiss me back, using his hands to caress my nipples, which causes my pleasure to spike through my body again. Then one of his arms wraps around my waist whilst the other hand is playing deliciously with one of my breasts, and he holds me still whilst thrusting up into me. My God, I'm shamelessly coming again! I hear him swear under his breath as he grabs my hips and thrusts harder into me until I feel him come inside me.

We sit breathless for a minute before he kisses my neck and unties my restraints. It's the drawstring from his shorts. *Resourceful,* I think, giggling. He rubs my wrists and kisses them. I didn't realise they felt sore until he did that.

Ed notices the moisturiser on my bedside table and applies some to my wrists. He lays down next to me, locking his eyes with mine. The intensity makes me think he's searching my eyes for something. I stroke his face and kiss him gently.

Chapter Nine

ED

I wake up around six in the morning, and it takes me a few minutes to realise where I am. I fell into such a deep sleep last night that I forgot I didn't leave Kiera's bed. She's lying next to me. I move her hair from her face so I can see her. She's absolutely breath-taking. I stroke her cheek with the back of my hand before I inspect her wrists. They look a little sore, so I grab the moisturiser from the bedside table and rub some of the cool cream in. I feel a little ashamed I lost it last night, but hearing her on the phone was my undoing. I had to have her, to make her come. I kept most of my control last night. In my experience, not many women appreciate being controlled in the bedroom. Kiera, on the other hand, may be different. The way her body responded to mine was pure ecstasy.

I pull on my shorts and leave her a note before heading out for my morning run. I can't run as hard as I normally push myself, but then it's been a while since

I've been able to have a session like last night. My muscles are like jelly from the orgasms and tense as hell from the positions we were in. I power walk the rest of the way home to shower and change for work, deciding to work from home today so I can check on Kiera later. I have a feeling she won't be resting like I told her.

By the time I've changed into my jeans and t-shirt, it's just gone eight. I give her a call to make sure she's up for work. I lost count of how many orgasms she had last night; I want to have her like that again, but in front of a mirror to watch her face. The thought of it has me stirring. I adjust my throbbing cock in my jeans, and Kiera doesn't answer. It's going to voicemail. Since I didn't have a key to lock her door this morning, I grab my laptop, phone and keys and head over to hers.

I feel rude letting myself into her flat, but I enter quietly and take in her space. Her kitchen and living area are open yet cosy. I notice two doors; one is her bedroom, which is wide open, and the other is the bathroom, where I hear the shower running. Luckily, I've packed an extra bandage just in case. I try to see where she can work and notice her laptop on her kitchen counter, but I don't see a stool. She can't work standing up with a swollen ankle.

The bathroom door opens, and I hear her say, "Jesus!" She hobbles out a moment later.

"Morning, sunshine." I grin at her.

"What are you doing here?"

"I wanted to make sure you were okay after your ankle and…last night."

Her face flushes. "I'm alright. I took the bandage off to shower, but I'm okay." She smiles.

"Can I strap you up again?" I laugh a little, thinking about both her ankle and her wrists. I don't normally let women see that side of me the first time, but Kiera has released something in me.

Kiera limps to her bedroom without answering me. I hear "Shit!" and assume she's hurt herself. She then pops her head round her door. "You coming then or what?" She winks at me.

I strap her ankle again. It feels as intimate as yesterday, but the chemistry has changed. Instead of it feeling too heavy with anticipation, there's a different current today, almost comfortable but still charged. We've slept with each other and shared a little more than a flirt. I want to kiss every inch of her, and I'm very tempted not to hold back because she's happy to see me even after I showed her a small part of my dark side.

As I'm deep in thought, she presents her wrists with a wink. I immediately want to take her, but I know we don't have time for that this morning. Instead, I rub her wrists with some more balm to help soothe any remaining soreness.

"Right, then. Let's talk about your working arrangements."

"The kitchen. Closer to food, drink and caffeine." She cocks her head and offers me a smile.

"There's no sign of any chair for you to rest your ankle. You're coming to mine to work for the day. There is food, drink and caffeine there, too. More importantly, you have someone to fetch those things for you, and you can rest whilst working. But we've got to get a shift on." I pointedly look at my watch. It's already eight-thirty.

Kiera rolls her eyes at me and gets up to get dressed. I smack her ass. "Roll those eyes at me again, and I'll take you over my knee, young lady." Her eyes widen with a glint of arousal. She bites her bottom lip and rolls her eyes again, giggling as she hobbles away quickly. I get up and grab her by the waist, spin her round gently, pulling her weight on me so she doesn't hurt her ankle, and kiss her. "You're lucky we've got to work this morning, but I won't forget." I wink at her and help her find clothes to wear.

We finally make it to mine just before nine. I set Kiera up at one end of my desk in my office. Because I work from home often, I've made my office comfortable with lots of space to work. I get Kiera a footstool and chair so she can work comfortably at my L-shaped desk.

"Sit." I feel my commanding voice come out, but she sits, no eye-rolling.

I make us a cuppa and some breakfast and walk back into the office. Her feet are on the floor. I set her cup of tea and breakfast in front of her and look at her.

She immediately puts her foot up, grinning at me. "You're such a Mr bossy pants, aren't you? Are you used to getting your own way?"

I laugh whilst sitting down in my chair. I've logged on but swivel around to face her. "Yes, but I can see you're going to give me trouble." I flash her a smile and get on with my work. I can already hear Kiera tapping on her keyboard. "Don't forget to eat." I can practically hear her roll her eyes at me. "I heard that eye roll. That's two for two over my knee."

She giggles and carries on with her typing.

Chapter Ten

KIERA

I wake up feeling sore, and my brain provides flashbacks of last night. I turn over to find Ed gone and a note on the pillow where he slept.

Kiera,

I'm sorry I lost control, but I'm not sorry I came over. Work from home, keep your ankle up and moisturise those wrists. I'll come by to check on you later.

Ed

The memory sends shivers down my spine—the way he completely dominated me and the way I let him. I enjoyed every moment and would gladly do it again. Checking my wrists, I notice they look freshly moisturised, then glance at the bottle on my bed. He took care of me before leaving. I want to say that's sweet, but that sentiment doesn't seem to fit.

I limp to the shower, and my ankle is in absolute agony, but as I take my bandage off, I remember wanting him to run his hand up my leg, which makes my skin tingle. My shower takes a little longer because I have to keep leaning on the tiles for support. However, when I get out of the bathroom, completely absorbed in my own little world, I about have a heart attack. There he is, standing in my living room, wearing black jeans and t-shirt. His brow is furrowed, making him appear concerned, but his eyes have wrinkles at the sides, making him look amused at the same time.

After a short, very bossy discussion about my working arrangements, we're at his place. I was only here briefly yesterday and never did get my tour. But from what I can see, his place is a lot more spacious than mine. He's got a larger living room and kitchen area with room for a dining table. He also has two bedrooms, one of which is an office, and a bigger bathroom. There's so much more light in here, too.

I sit at the end of his desk in my own chair and am made to put my foot up. He wasn't joking about the waiter service. I even have breakfast.

I email my boss and say I'm working from home today due to a twisted ankle. I get a response telling me to work the morning to finish up a strategy plan and then take the remainder of the day to rest. I'm not going to say no to that.

Before I know it, I finish my strategy plan and send it to the team to add their pieces where relevant. I'm now leaning back, listening to Ed on one of his calls. It seems his bossiness doesn't stay at home.

"…Yes, Janet. I understand that you have other commitments, but if I ask for something to be done, I expect it to be done on time. I gave you a week to carry out an hour's worth of work. I expect it to be in my inbox by the morning." He hangs up, running his fingers through his hair. I flush, remembering my hands in his hair last night and then his in mine.

He spins round and catches me watching him. A smile slowly spreads across his face as he wheels over to me. "Are we done for the day, missy?" he says, leaning back in his chair and crossing his arms.

"As a matter of fact, Mr bossy pants, I am. My boss gave me the afternoon to rest. So, I might hobble home, order some food and veg on the sofa for the rest of the day." As I speak, I look forward to the idea, yet want to stay here, too. It is a very odd feeling. I enjoy vegging out on the sofa and doing nothing, but I also want to spend more time with Ed. I thoroughly enjoy his company as well as the extra activities.

"Here's a counteroffer. How about you stay here, order food and veg on my sofa for the afternoon? That way, I can make sure your ankle is okay. I get to enjoy having you around more, and there's less travel involved for me to deliver your punishment later." He winks at me, and my breath catches. I know he threatened to take me over his knee, but he wouldn't. Would he?

I blush, picturing him bending me over and spanking me. I get a rush of tingles throughout my body like an electric current. He's staring at me again, stroking his stubble, giving me a dirty smile. He's definitely going to do it. I tempt fate and roll my eyes as I stand up to stumble into his living room.

"Right, that's it. Three for three!" He stands swiftly and slings me over his shoulder like I weigh nothing more than a sack of potatoes, making me squeal in delight. He swats my ass as we walk out of the office. "I warned you, missy," he says in his dark voice that sends shivers down my spine.

"Well, I didn't think you'd actually go through with it." I can't stop giggling. The thought of being spanked is one of those taboo fantasies I've had but never thought I'd enjoy. But I also didn't think I'd like being tied up and dominated, and although I feel as though last night was a light demonstration, I thoroughly enjoyed it.

Ed sits down on the sofa, lowering me to perch next to him. He looks at me and pushes my hair away from my face. "Ready?" I bite my lip, not really knowing what to expect. He lays me over his knee, and I start to giggle again from nervousness and anticipation.

Ed smoothly runs his hand over my ass, and right after his hand leaves it, I feel it smack me gently. I let out a noise that sounds like I'm starring in a PornHub film, which I wasn't expecting. Who knew spanking would actually turn me on a little? He strokes my ass again, and then down comes his hand on my other cheek. I moan a little louder this time; I felt it right in my sweet spot. He said three for three, right? One more to go, and this one hits with a smacking noise, making me feel the sting and the pleasure at once. He pats my ass lightly and lifts me back up.

"Next time, we'll try with beads or eggs in," he says with a smirk before kissing me hard. I've heard of beads before, but eggs? I'm going to have to do some research later when he's working. When we come up for air, I see fire in his eyes. This man is horny as hell, and I love it. I shift to straddle him and lower my face to kiss him but decide to hover long enough to tease him. A low growl vibrates from his body as he moves his hands to my hips. I can see he's fighting with his control; his body is tense, and his fingers are almost bruising my skin. He wants to take over, and I might just let him.

Chapter Eleven

ED

This woman drives me crazy. We've gone from an easy friendship to amazing sex, caring and teasing within a few weeks. She's testing her boundaries by rolling her eyes at me, and I've spanked her arse to show her I will do it. Now, she's on top of me, testing my control, hovering over my mouth, teasing me with those gorgeous lips. I hold onto her hips to stop myself from taking over.

It looks like she's thinking about something, but I can't tell what it is. Kiera's cheeky grin appears. She leans back and places her hands behind her back whilst simultaneously grinding herself against my hardening cock. I'm done. I used to have so much control when I was with other women, but this one…this one brings out my other side and seems to enjoy it. The moment she doesn't like anything we are doing, we'll stop. We discussed safe words and limits previously. She chose red as her safe word.

I grab her hips, lift her off me and place her on the sofa. "Stay put," I order as I walk into the bedroom. When I return, her eyebrows are pulled down together, and she's hugging her legs, making her look a little sad, but she is still biting that lip. "Hey, what's wrong? Kiera?"

"Did I do something wrong?" She's staring down at her feet.

Oh crap. I did something wrong. "No, I went to get these." I produce two ties, and her eyes light up again.

"Stop biting that lip, or I'm going to do it for you." I can hear my deeper voice coming out and see her squirm in her seat. Can she really take the darker side of me?

"Stop making threats and get over here already." She grins, and I can't move quickly enough.

I take her lip in my mouth to suck and nibble on it before bringing her hands in front of her and binding them together. She cocks her head to one side, her eyes locking onto the second tie, almost as if she's asking where it's going. I cover her eyes and knot it around the back of her head. I stand back and admire the woman sitting in front of me. I'm no professional Dom, but I do enjoy dominating and light bondage. Kiera's body is trembling slightly, and her breathing is shallow, so I lower myself to her, reminding her of the safe word. Her other senses should be heightened with her eyes covered.

I blow on her ear a little, which makes her jump, and I chuckle whilst tracing her collarbone lightly with my fingertip. This makes her twitch. Her breathing is getting heavier, and she's biting her lip.

Using my thumb, I pull her lip free from her teeth and rub it. Her lips have parted slightly, and my God, she's going to make me come from seeing her like this. I kneel in front of her and kiss her jaw. Kiera jolts slightly and gasps, leaning her head to give me more access to her neck. "Good girl." I nibble and suck on the delicate area of her neck, making her sigh with pleasure. I can see her nipples showing through her bra.

I'm working my way to you, ladies. Don't worry.

I raise her arms up over her head and bend her elbows so she doesn't get achy, pulling her boobs up in the process. Lifting her top, I begin to kiss her stomach and slowly make my way up to her pert nipples, finding a wonderful surprise—a front-clasp bra. Makes for much easier work to set these babies free. I unhook her bra and gently take each nipple in my mouth in turn. Kiera throws her head back, and I can feel the vibrations of the noises she is making before I hear them. I lean back slightly and blow cool air onto her breasts, immediately taking one nipple in my mouth again whilst tweaking the other with my finger and thumb.

I tease her jeans down along with her knickers to check her wetness. I can smell her arousal, and I can't believe how hard I'm getting. I push her legs apart and trail kisses up her thighs. It makes me smile thinking about how turned on she is. I quickly check my watch; I've got forty-five minutes until my next meeting. We're going to have to be quick, though I could spend all day on Kiera.

I lean back, taking her in. She is sitting on my sofa, hands bound and blindfolded, panting and squirming slightly. She bites her bottom lip again. I reach up and pull it from her teeth, leaning in for a kiss. It starts out slow and tender, becoming more passionate as she reacts. I come up for air and trail my tongue down from her ear to her neck whilst pushing my trousers down. I pull her hips towards me, ensuring most of her weight is supported by the sofa and thrust into her as I bite down on her neck. The noise that comes from her is purely primal. I love it! I hold her hips tightly, keeping her as close to me as possible with each thrust, going deeper each time, and my God, she feels like she is continuously coming. Before Kiera, I had restraint with women; I lasted for hours. This woman has flipped a switch in me that is making me come after ten minutes.

I pull her blindfold up onto her forehead, and she blinks, getting used to the light again. "You okay?" I ask, concern lacing my voice.

"Um, hum…Yea, I mean…Yea…" She giggles, slightly dazed. Thank God.

Moving closer again, I kiss her gently, searching her eyes for any fear, regret, or worry. I see none of those emotions. I'm not sure what I'm seeing, but I hope it's happiness.

"You gonna stare all day or let me sit a little more dignified." She's laughing as she wriggles her hips back to sit more upright.

"I was going to leave you tied up, but sure, I'll let you get dressed." I wink at her, untying her wrists. They don't look marked, but I still rub them with some moisturiser, kissing them afterwards.

Once she is more dignified, as she puts it, I show her round the apartment and order us some lunch. After Kiera is settled on the sofa with a panini and iced tea, I return to my office.

The rest of the afternoon is meeting after meeting. In between them, I make a cup of coffee and check on Kiera. After five, I finally finish for the day and feel exhausted. I head into the living room and see Kiera fast asleep on the sofa. She is snoring, which is cute. That is until a noise that I can only describe as like a dragon emerging from a cave before it breathes fire comes out of her, and I burst out laughing. I've not had many serious relationships, and I rarely let women sleep over, so this is new to me, and I find myself enjoying the view.

Chapter Twelve

KIERA

I wake to the sound of laughter; I didn't realise I had fallen asleep. It takes me a few minutes to adjust to my surroundings again. I'm at Ed's, had some awesome orgasms, lunch and apparently a nap. I glance up at him. His arms are folded across his chest, and his lips are turned up into a smug smile as laughter dances in his eyes. He's handsome.

"What?" I say, still slightly groggy, with a smile.

"You sound like you're a demon when you snore." He laughs and walks into the kitchen, saying he's going to grab us both a glass of water.

"Well, yes, I do," I say, fighting back a laugh. There's no denying it. My mum used to say it's me announcing I'm asleep and happy when I snore.

"How's the ankle?"

I had completely forgotten about it, so it must be feeling better. "It's absolutely fine. Haven't felt it all afternoon, which means I can get out of your hair." I feel a strange pull in my chest again as I say those words. I want to go home because I don't want to be a nuisance or look like I'm being too clingy too fast, but I want to stay with him because he's easy to be around. We're friends who have had sex. I don't want to mess up our friendship or whatever this new development is by moving too quickly or overstaying my welcome.

"Nonsense. Stay for dinner, and I'll walk you home. How's that?" He smiles at me sweetly.

"Okay then. What are we having?" I'm suddenly hungry again, but I did burn off some extra calories before lunch and then had a nap.

Ed returns to the kitchen, goes through his cupboards and fridge, and then announces we're having chicken pesto pasta for dinner. My stomach rumbles in agreement.

I hobble, a little more easily than I did this morning, over to the kitchen and lean against the countertop. "What can I help with?"

"You can sit." He pulls out a bar stool for me to sit on whilst he works around the kitchen.

I do as he says and watch as he moves about. He's making his own pesto, which is quite impressive. He dips a spoon in and gives it to me to taste. "So much better than the jar ones." My stomach growls, which makes him laugh.

We sit at the breakfast bar to eat dinner. Chicken pesto pasta is now one of my favourite dishes. After dinner, I try to help wash up, but Ed shoos me to the sofa. It is another hour before we walk back to my flat. The stroll is as comfortable as it has been since we first met, but there's something unspoken between us. It's been a crazy twenty-four hours, and I wouldn't change it.

Ed helps me up the steps and gives me a kiss on the cheek before heading back home. I enter my flat and plonk myself down on the sofa. I text Jess to see if she's free for a chat. I need to talk through the last couple of weeks. When Jess tells me she's free in an hour, I decide to have a quick shower and make a cuppa. My phone rings whilst I'm scrolling through social media.

"Hey, stranger. How you doing?" Jess sounds light and happy. I know she's enjoying life with Gavin and thriving in her new job.

"Not bad. You sound happy!"

"I am really happy. But before we drown ourselves in gossip about my love life, what's going on with you?"

"I think I met someone."

"Think? Is he real?" Jess laughs, but I know she wants all the details.

"Well, the night I told you I met that hot stranger at the bar, it turns out he lives in the same area. We've been bumping into each other and texting a lot. He saved me from an absolutely appalling date, and we ended up having dinner together." I suddenly feel nervous about telling her what happened next.

"Kiera, you okay?"

"Yeah. Anyway, on the way home last night, I was clumsy and twisted my ankle. We were outside his, and he took me up to strap my ankle. There was a heavy feeling around us. Like that atmospheric change right before a good thunderstorm."

"Ooohhh! This is going to be JUICY!" She giggled.

"Well, one thing led to another, and we ended up having the most amazing sex at mine, and this morning, he ordered me to work from his place."

"Ordered?"

"He's a little domineering but sweet at the same time. It's hard to describe, but it's hot as hell. We ended up having more awesome sex, and then he bought me home tonight after cooking me dinner. I have butterflies when I think about him, and honestly, when he touches me, it feels like he leaves a trail of fire on my skin."

Jess was silent for a moment and then exhaled loudly. "Kiera, you're in so much trouble."

"Care to elaborate?"

"It sounds like you're catching feelings for him. I've never heard you describe sex as amazing. Do you feel safe with him?"

"Absolutely! It feels like I'm protected when I'm with him. I feel alive. You know, I thought I was broken down there, especially after hearing about your sexcapades!" I laughed. "It's like he woke me up, if that makes any sense. Do I sound crazy?"

"Not at all. You know how it is with me and Gavin. It was like a sexual awakening as well as a personal one. I'm obviously going to have to meet him if he's made you feel like this after a matter of weeks."

"I have no idea what this is, so I'm not going to launch the best friend idea on him yet. We'll see where it goes, and then you can meet him."

"Fine, I'll agonisingly wait to torture some poor man." She laughs, but I also know she wants to check him out sooner rather than later. We sit and chat for a good hour or so about anything and everything.

We say our goodbyes with a promise to meet up soon, and I wander into the kitchen to make another cuppa. I decide a cup of tea in bed with a book is how I'm going to spend the rest of the night. I get about five chapters in before I'm fast asleep.

Chapter Thirteen

ED

The darkness has taken me yet again. I'm curled in a corner after receiving my latest beating from him. The pain is spreading through my back, where I take a lot of the kicks. I'm winded and struggling to breathe, but my heart is beating faster from fear. I can hear my mum shouting at us from downstairs that dinner is almost ready.

"You say anything to her, and next time, I'll kill you."

Shame overwhelms me as I slowly uncurl and do a mental check of the pain. I head downstairs, and everything goes black.

I wake up in a cold sweat. It's been a few months since I had a nightmare like that. It may have something to do with the family BBQ my mum insists I go to this weekend. Memories of my childhood haunt me, but my childhood is what has made me the man I am today. I need to be in control of everything because I spent too many years without having any control… with others controlling me.

I haven't had a long-term relationship since I was

in my early twenties. I woke up one night after a nightmare, and it freaked my girlfriend out. We stayed together for a few months after that, but she didn't want to deal with any drama or trauma.

I spent years in counselling after that, needing to get a handle on my past and face my demons, but I don't feel like the counsellor helped me. Every now and then, though, I'm still taunted with nightmares.

It's six in the morning, so I get up and take a shower to reset myself. With the water running over me, I push my nightmare out and let it run down the drain, feeling a little lighter. My thoughts then move to Kiera. The lightness that is around her is infectious. I feel brighter with her, but I don't want to dim her sunny charm with my darkness.

Dressed and standing in the kitchen with a coffee after my shower, I decide to skip my morning run today, even though it will probably clear my head. My thoughts drift to Kiera again. Thinking about the last couple of days, I feel my insecurities rise. Have I scared her off? Was I too controlling? Why am I this caught up?

I think about this weekend and feel nauseous. How am I going to get through a family gathering with him there? I normally pick a girl for the weekend and take her as my buffer, but I don't want to this time. I mean, I want a buffer, but I don't want a random girl. This thing with Kiera—whatever it is—is drawing me in. Would she want to go with me? I mean, it's a bit early for "meet the parents" since we don't even know what this is between us.

Suck it up, Ed. Text her to see how she is, then casually mention there's a BBQ on Sunday, and you'd like her to join you if she's free. She may just say yes because there's food.

Pulling out my phone, I take a deep breath and begin to type.

> Me: Hey, how you feeling today?

There, I sent her a message and will anxiously wait for her response. I've got a lot to do today, so I decide to work from home instead of going into the office. I'm not feeling peopley today.

After checking my emails, I hear my phone ping. It's about eight o'clock.

> Kiera: Not bad. Ankle is a lot better. Working from home today, and before you get all Mr bossy pants, I'm going to be sitting on the sofa after doing a couple of laps of the kitchen, and yes…I'm rolling my eyes right now.

I can't help but laugh. Her humour is wonderful. She understands some of my controlling behaviour, but she still likes to push the boundaries. It's refreshing. Not many of the women I've slept with have seen that side of me. I show them a little and see judgment in their eyes, so I haven't let it out much. With her, it's front and centre. She hasn't run away—not that she can with her ankle, so there's a bonus.

Me: Ha-ha! If you can hobble over, you're welcome to use my desk again.

Kiera: You're not in the office today?

Me: No, didn't feel peopley today. I have left over pasta if that will entice you? Lol.

Kiera: Are you trying to say my working conditions aren't up to your standards, Mr BP?

Me: I can't see your H&S team signing off on that either, let's face it!

Kiera: I rolled my eyes so hard at that comment.

Me: You know what happens when you roll your eyes at me, missy.

Kiera: I honestly don't know what you're talking about.

I can hear her in my head laughing as she's typing her replies. Is she teasing me? Testing my reaction? Does she enjoy it? I mean, the sounds that came out of her over the last couple of days make it seem as if she does. Whilst I'm lost in my thoughts, I hear a knock at the door. Strange, no one has buzzed up. I walk over and look through the peephole, and there she is, my ray of sunshine to blast away the darkness. I open the door with a sly smile on my face, and she walks right on in as if she lives here. I love it.

"I couldn't sit there knowing I was going against all sorts of health and safety rules and whatnot, Mr Bossy Pants. You gonna help a girl get set up?" She grins as she hobbles into my office. I notice she's putting more weight on her ankle, which is good.

I follow her like a lost puppy dog. She's setting herself up in the same spot as yesterday, and I lean against the door frame, watching. Her hair is up in a messy bun today, and she is wearing shorts and a vest that shows off her lovely tan. She glances up at me with an easy, pure smile that melts away the remaining bad memories. I walk back into the kitchen and set about making her a cuppa and some snacks.

The morning flies by. Our calls and work have kept us both busy until well past lunch. Hearing her stomach rumble wakes mine up. I order us some food from a local deli, but since she's still on a call, I hazard a guess as to what she's fancying. Lunch arrives forty minutes later. Luckily, her call has finished. Placing her food in front of her, I see her eyes light up.

"Ooh, what do we have for lunch?"

"I ordered us today's special, chicken and chorizo salad." My mouth is practically watering just saying it.

Kiera tucks in, devouring her lunch like it's the last meal she'll eat.

Chapter Fourteen

KIERA

There's something different with Ed today. He seems distracted, and although I came over to work, he's got a different energy about him. He normally acts free and easy, but today, he seems sad. I don't want to pry, but I'm eager to see if he will tell me what's bothering him.

Our day flashes in the blink of an eye. He treats me to lunch, which is gorgeous, then we work solidly throughout the afternoon. Yesterday, we had fun and talked throughout the day, but today has been quiet.

As five o'clock rolls in, I shut down my laptop and sit back, observing Ed as he concentrates on the colourful graph on his screen. "What time do you finish, Mr Bossy Pants?" I'm acting sassy to see if he will smile.

"Just a few more minutes, and I'm done." He doesn't turn around, but his voice is devoid of emotion. I watch as he types and finally shuts down his laptop.

He turns to me with a grim twist to the mouth, his eyes avoiding mine.

"Are you going to keep pretending something isn't bothering you?" I ask with all the kindness and sincerity I can.

"That obvious, huh?" He gets up and gathers our cups. I'm left confused, but I limp after him, able to put more weight on my ankle now. Hopefully, over the weekend, it'll get a lot better, so I can go to the office on Monday. As much as I'm enjoying working with Ed, I miss the bustle of the office.

"You hungry?" he asks flatly as he washes our dishes.

"Ed…" I shuffle up behind him and put my hand on his shoulder. His body tenses. Have I done something wrong? But he looked happy to see me this morning, and he offered a spot at his desk. "Um, no, not hungry at the moment. I've got some bits to do at home, though, so I'll head off. Thank you for today. It's nice to have company."

I go into the office to gather my things, and he's there in the doorway, staring at me. His eyes appear darker, not in a threatening way, but I'm not sure what is behind them. He sighs heavily, keeping his arms close to his body, somehow making him appear smaller.

"I'm sorry. I've not been a very good host. You don't have to leave."

"You seem to be going through something. I can stay if you want to talk it out. Whatever it is, it's eating you up inside. But I can also go so you have some headspace to talk to your demons." His eyes widen at the word demons, and the vein in his neck pulses against his now ashen skin. Bingo! That's what he's been dealing with today.

I can see the internal struggle he is having. His shoulders are tense, and there's a slight tremor in his arms. It's so slight that I almost miss it and the small bead of sweat on his forehead. Is he afraid?

I walk up to him, trying to limp a little less so he doesn't feel like he has to look after me. I place my hand on his shoulder and kiss him on the cheek. "Catch you later?" I say before I leave. Something inside me wants to hold him, to draw out whatever has caused his mood today and to make it better. But I also know that if he wants to tell me, he will.

Later, I'm in my kitchen eating crackers that have been in the cupboard too long. They're a little stale, but they'll do. I left Ed's a couple of hours ago and still feel guilty about leaving him alone with his demons. I decide to text him to see if he's okay.

> Me: Have you made friends with your demons yet?

I can see those three dots appear, disappear and come back again. When nothing comes through in the ten minutes I've been staring at my phone, I decide to treat myself to a bath. Jess gave me some of those magic salts that are meant to help you relax, so I thought I'd give them a go. I pour myself a glass of wine whilst I'm running the bath, wandering around in nothing but my silk robe. Just as I'm about to get into the bath, my door buzzer sounds.

Rolling my eyes, I stagger over to it. No one drops by. Why is it the one time I choose to chill in a bath, someone comes over? "Hello?"

"It's me. Can I come up?" Ed sounds more defeated than he did earlier. I buzz him up and open the door whilst I head to the kitchen to pour him a glass of wine. Something tells me he needs a drink.

Ed walks in. He seems smaller than usual. Whatever is going on in his head has really gotten to him. I offer him the glass of wine, and he gives me a weak smile in return.

"I was just about to get in the bath. Come in and chat whilst I pretend the magic salts are working." I laugh, and he brightens a little. He follows me into the bathroom and watches as I get in the bath.

He dips his hand in, yanking it out and looking at me concerned. "What is it with women and getting into water that's hotter than molten lava?" Shaking his head, he chuckles, but it sounds forced. It's not as carefree as his normal laugh.

I wink and get in, humming when the warmth surrounds me. He shakes his head and sits down on the floor, leaning against the wall, facing me. I sense he wants to talk, but I'm going to force it. I wait and drink my cold wine in my lava bath.

We sit for a few minutes in silence. Ed catches me staring at him a couple of times and diverts his gaze to the floor. He drapes his hand over the side of the bath and dips his fingers in, looking at me with a small smile on his face. "Still the temperature of hell."

"Ed, we've not known each other long, but I can tell something is getting you down today. Do you want to talk about it?" I eventually say. It bugs me that something has clearly upset him.

He peers up at me with such sadness in his eyes and drinks the rest of his wine. He gets up and steps out of the bathroom.

Chapter Fifteen

ED

I feel the darkness taking hold of me when Kiera leaves after we finish working. I sit on the sofa and don't notice nearly two hours have gone by because I'm deep in my head, re-living my past. After, I get up and go for a walk. I don't know where I'm going, but it's better than moping around my apartment all night.

I end up at her door, her gravity pulling me towards her. She buzzes me in, and I sit on her bathroom floor in silence whilst she soaks in a bath. I'm laughing internally at how hot it is. I'd need to wait a good hour for it to cool down before I could get in.

Kiera asks if I want to talk about what's upset me. I want to talk to her; I feel like I need to let someone in. No one knows anything about my childhood, not even my own mum. I feel like she has suspected, but she never did or said anything.

I get up and head to the kitchen after I down the remaining wine in my glass. We're going to need a bottle for this. Returning to the bathroom, her eyes are on me. She looks apprehensive but offers me a smile that doesn't reach her eyes. I feel like my darkness has already dimmed some of her bright light. Should I let her in? I don't want her consumed. I sit back down and refill our glasses. Why am I so comfortable being with her? I've known her for a matter of weeks, and I'm sitting in her bathroom whilst she's in the bath. This is a new level of friendship for me. Most of my friends are from work, and I didn't have many as I was growing up, but I also wasn't a carefree kid who easily made friends.

I stare at her for a moment before I make my decision. "I had a nightmare last night," I practically whisper. The wave of embarrassment that comes over me makes me divert my gaze from hers. She doesn't say anything.

"I didn't have a normal childhood. Well, I did from the nuclear family perspective, but that's where it ends." I glance up, waiting for the feeling of regret to drown me, but all I see is concern and patience in Kiera's eyes, so I continue anxiously, "I have an older brother, Noel. He's four years older than me. I remember being a small child, toddler age when it first started."

I hear water sloshing and see Kiera getting out of the bath and wrapping a towel around her. She sits next to me on the floor. I watch her warily, and I'm honestly scared about opening up. She puts one hand on my knee, the other holding her wine, and it gives me a small bit of courage. "I was pushed down the stairs by my brother. I clearly remember the look in his eyes. He was grinning down at me when I landed at the bottom of the stairs and glared at me when I sat up crying. I felt scared of him from that moment on."

My hands begin to shake. Kiera silently takes one of my hands in hers, lacing her fingers through mine and squeezing. Still watching me as I talk, she nods her head and purses her lips as she raises her eyebrows in concern.

"After that, it was almost daily. My mum would say I was incredibly clumsy, but I wasn't. I'd 'walk into things' a lot, apparently. Of course, it had nothing to do with my brother throwing toys at me to see which would hurt the most, more accidents on the stairs, or being pushed into walls and door frames. It got worse when I got older and could talk. He would threaten me, saying if I told anyone, he would kill me. I believed him, so I never told anyone. Ever."

Kiera's expression has changed. She no longer looks concerned; she looks angry. Her nostrils are flaring, and she is grinding her teeth. She tightens her grip on my hand, her jaw relaxing, and she is visibly calming herself down.

This small action allows me to continue and makes me feel safe. "Three ribs were broken when I was four. My elbow has come out of its socket more times than I can count. After the eighth visit to the hospital, the doctors were growing concerned about abuse. She told them I was clumsy and got into a lot of accidents. I think she knew something else was going on but didn't want to admit it.

"When I was nine, Noel was thirteen. He'd grown stronger. His beatings lasted longer and hurt a lot more. He was more careful after the doctors got suspicious, though. I had less serious injuries but a lot more minor ones. This all carried on until he left for uni. I felt a little safer after that, but the conditioning had already taken over. I didn't have friends, nor did I speak to my mum or dad much. I concentrated on schoolwork as a form of escape. When he would come home during holidays, it all started again. I decided to leave home at seventeen. I couldn't cope anymore. My parents helped me get my first flat since I didn't have any income, but as soon as I got a job and started working my way up, I paid them back. I didn't want to be a burden on them." I can feel the tears threatening to fall, and I keep staring at the floor.

"From as far back as I can remember, whenever I got hurt, I went to a dark place in my mind. It was literally pitch black with his voice surrounding, taunting and threatening me. That's where I ended up in my nightmare last night. It was a flashback to one of the beatings, and then everything went black. I've not been able to shake this feeling all day. No one noticed before because my mask has always been firmly in place. But you…you saw right through it."

I summon the courage to look at Kiera. She's angry and has tears in her eyes. Her hold on my hand is dangerously close to cutting off my circulation. She puts down her wine, grabs mine and sets both on the floor before engulfing me in the strongest hug I've ever experienced. Tears are falling down my face, and I am shaking. I'm not used to this. I've always received love from my parents, don't get me wrong, but I've never been held like this, not that I can remember anyway.

We continue to hug for a few minutes. She pulls back and wipes my tears away with her thumbs. "I'm so sorry you went through that. Thank you for trusting me." She opens and closes her mouth a few times as if she is stopping herself from saying something. "If I ever have the displeasure of meeting your brother, I'm going to make him regret what he did to you." Her eyes have darkened, and she has narrowed as she speaks. She takes in a deep breath, and her light looks brighter. It is a very strange combination, one that I am shocked to realize very much arouses me.

"Well, now that you mention it…"

Chapter Sixteen

KIERA

The anger brewing inside of me is nothing I have ever felt. I've been pissed off before, but this… this is all-consuming. My mind races with all the things I want to do to Ed's brother. My thoughts are dark, and I've never had these types of thoughts before. It's like a switch has been flipped, and it's slightly concerning. When Jess suggested I was "catching feelings," she may have been right. Ed is lovely, kind, and funny. He is easy to be with and has made me feel things I didn't think were possible.

After hearing about his childhood, I felt his pain throughout my body. I want to wrap him up and protect him. He's more than capable of doing that for himself, I'm sure, but I feel very angry that someone hurt him. No, not someone, his own brother. I issue a threat, but I'm probably never going to get the chance to go through with it; however, something dark inside me wants to carry out my every thought.

"Well, now that you mention it…" Ed looks at me sheepishly. "My mum's having a family gathering this weekend and wants me to go. I used to take a 'buffer girl' to these things, but I didn't want to this time. I think the thought of me being there alone is what triggered the nightmare."

"When is it?"

"Sunday lunchtime."

"I'm coming with you. If you want me there, of course." I smile. It's not a happy smile; it's a little more sadistic as I think of ways to break his brother mentally. I feel the muscle ticking in my jaw. I notice Ed staring at me, and his eyebrows are drawn together as he tilts his head to one side, blinking slowly.

"You look darker than normal. I'm sorry—"

"I can handle it. I'm angry on your behalf." I'm currently fantasizing about his brother's demise, but I don't verbalise this. Maybe I am a little darker than normal.

We sit on the bathroom floor for a while longer before my legs become numb. I get up and pull him with me. "I'm going to change, and then we're going to move to a more comfortable seating arrangement." I laugh as I walk to my bedroom. By the time I come out, Ed has made us both a cuppa and is sitting on the couch, lost in his thoughts.

I sit next to him, grab my cup and sip my coffee. Normally, I drink coffee during the day and tea at night, but I was enjoying the extra caffeine hit this evening. I sit patiently, waiting for him to speak first. I feel a wave of emotions. He trusted me enough to tell me about his past and his nightmare, and he feels comfortable sitting with me afterwards. I want to reassure him that it doesn't make me think any differently of him, but it does. He's strong. I couldn't have coped with that type of abuse. I wonder if that's why he likes control now. It's not something I'm scared of based on the couple of times we've had sex. In fact, I've loved allowing him to be in charge.

It's been fifteen minutes, but he's not talking yet. So, I thought I'd make the first move. "How do you feel now that you've told someone about it?" I'm nervous about his reply. What if he regrets talking to me?

He glances at me. His green eyes, although darker in colour, seem brighter. It may be the tears that have caused that, though. My eyes always appear to sparkle after a good cry session.

"Thank you for listening, for not judging, and for wanting to come with me this weekend. It's a lot to put on you in one night. I understand if you change your mind at any point." Ed goes back to avoiding eye contact.

I put my cup down and move closer, practically sitting on him. I grab his face and gently lift his gaze up to me. "Ed, you trusted me with something so private tonight. Of course, I'm coming on Sunday to be your buffer." He smiles briefly. "Although, I cannot be held responsible for my mouth if he starts on you at the party." I wink, and he laughs.

"I would love to see someone stand up to him. I'm ashamed it hasn't been me."

"Don't you do that. You'll have your chance. You need to face your demons before you can use them against someone." I pull him into me, not wanting to let him go. I feel him relax.

We sit like this for a while, and I notice it's gone midnight. I stand up and grab his hand, taking him to my bedroom. He needs to be cared for tonight. He doesn't say a word as he follows me and undresses down to his boxers. Lying down, I cuddle him. He's letting me be the big spoon, which I'm grateful for, and I stay awake long enough to hear his soft snores before I drift off into my own little dreamland, telling my subconscious to not let him go.

IT'S NEARLY MIDDAY WHEN I FINALLY DRAG MY ASS OUT of bed. It took me a moment to remember Ed should be here somewhere. I look at his side, and there isn't a note. I head to the bathroom before going to make a coffee. When I walk out, I see Ed on my sofa reading something on his phone. I smile at him; he looks better. Lighter even.

"Good afternoon, sunshine," he says, grinning, not lifting his gaze from his phone.

"How long have you been up?" I pull a cup out of the cupboard, wondering why I feel at ease with him. It's only been a few weeks since we've known each other.

"Only a couple of hours. That was the best sleep I've had in a long time." He's suddenly behind me, his hands on my hips, turning me. "Thank you." He looks into my eyes for a moment before kissing me.

My body tingles. His hand moves to my hair, holding it firmly. He breaks the kiss sooner than I would have liked. "You're walking around much better now." Ed smiles as he goes back to the couch to pick up his phone. I shake my head and carry on with the task I momentarily forgot.

It's five in the evening before I realise we've spent the day together chilling in my flat. Talking, music on in the background, he's been glued to his phone most of the afternoon. It has me wondering what he's been focused on for so long.

"Anything interesting?" I ask whilst nodding at his phone.

"Sorry, I've been researching." He appears sheepish.

"For five hours?" I chuckle and stop when he shows me his search. Counsellors that deal with childhood abuse trauma. I look at him with apologetic eyes.

"It's okay. Don't worry. I want to get a better handle on this if I'm going to use my demons." He winks at me and puts his phone on the table.

"We've barely eaten all day. Get up, shower and dress. We're going out." His tone is authoritative and makes me feel like an electric current is running through it. I can feel myself blushing, which makes his small smile grow into a devilish grin. As I get up, he smacks my ass. "And don't forget you told me you rolled your eyes at me, missy."

I laugh as I walk to the bathroom.

We hop on the tube and go into the city for dinner. Ed isn't giving me any indication about where he is taking me. As we walk from Oxford Circus, his hand is on the small of my back, directing me into a Mexican restaurant. The smell hits me as we step in, and my stomach is pleased.

We're seated at a table near the window. I love people-watching when I eat out, but I find myself focusing on Ed like we're the only people in the restaurant.

When the waiter comes over, Ed orders for the both of us. I raise my eyebrows and smirk. I'm seeing more of his controlling and domineering side, but it's not bad. I find myself wondering if I've missed some red flags along the line, but I feel safe with him and enjoy his company.

"What's got you smiling?" He winks at me, making my insides melt a little.

"Other than when jerk-off ordered my salad and the times you've ordered a few times for me, I've not had food ordered for me without consultation. How do you know I don't have any allergies?" I say teasingly, but the concern on his face makes me laugh.

"Good point. Do you have any?"

"Nope. Just wanted to make a point." I take a sip of the wine the waiter brought over and smile.

"I think we need to discuss what's happening here." He sounds serious. I simply nod and take another drink of wine.

Chapter Seventeen

ED

Watching Kiera in the restaurant makes me want to talk about what's happening between us. Since my last serious girlfriend, many moons ago, I haven't thought about another due to my past trauma and nightmares. But this woman, sitting across from me with her light showing, has me thinking it could be possible. With her.

When I bring the subject up, she nods and drinks. Is she uncomfortable?

"This is unexpected for me if I'm being honest. I wasn't looking for anything. We were building a great friendship, which led to more. I just want to know where you're at?" I sit back, gulping from my own glass. The waiter looks in my direction, and I raise my glass, signalling for more wine. I feel like we're going to need it.

"You know I've had a string of bad dates; I was

looking for something but never found it." She pauses, appearing deep in thought. We're momentarily distracted when more drinks come to our table, shortly followed by our food. Kiera beams at her plate and starts to eat.

I'm not sure if I can stomach my food right now, but I'm going to eat so I don't look awkward.

Halfway through her quesadilla, she glances at me. I'm trying to gauge her thoughts from her body language. She isn't acting any differently. That's got to be a good sign, right?

She continues to torture me throughout the meal. Once her stomach is satisfied, she makes eye contact, something I've been wanting since our food arrived. She smiles sweetly at me; the butterflies are back. I finish the remainder of my taco in an attempt to quiet down my growing anxiety. It does not help.

"Where do you see this going?" She spins it back on me. Clever. I guess she wants to see what I feel before saying anything further.

"We have a connection I've not experienced before. It's something I'd like to continue and explore further." I drink, pausing to gather my thoughts. I want to be careful how I word my next sentence. "I'm a possessive man, Kiera. If we're together, you're mine."

Her eyes widen. She bites her bottom lip, which makes me want to bite it for her, and she shifts in her seat. "Well then, looks like I'm yours." The emphasis she puts on that last word makes me want to get her home as quickly as possible. I signal for the bill, pay and practically drag her out of the restaurant.

We're back at mine after a painstakingly long tube ride. I swear it didn't take as long to get there as it did to get back. I'm leaning against the kitchen island, watching her watching me. The electricity in the air is thick. I put my water down and stalk over to her, not breaking eye contact. She's mine now. I talk through the things we've already done and what I'd like to explore with her. Ensuring that limits will be discussed each time before we start anything.

"Tell me if I get too rough," I whisper in her ear and feel her body shiver. "Give me your safe word."

Kiera looks at me, biting her lip and whispers back, "I'm changing it to peach." Her eyes are wide, and I can almost see the fire I feel whenever she kisses me.

"Okay." I grab her hand and lead her to my bedroom.

Since I left home, controlling everything has become a way of life, and I've discovered I enjoyed it in the bedroom. I love dominating, light bondage and making sure the woman I'm with experiences as much pleasure as possible. I did a lot of research before going there sexually. I had no interest in the S&M side, but I wanted to make sure I made my partners feel safe. I've only been able to lose control with one other woman. She wanted more from me, and I wasn't in a head-space to give it at the time. I've discussed the traffic light scale with Kiera, red for stop, yellow for not sure and green for go go go... We both know when to use our words.

As I stand at the foot of my bed, I move Kiera's hair from her neck to give me access. I kiss her just above her collarbone, and her head tilts to the side. "Good girl," I tell her and bite her. I can feel the goose-bumps on her arms. I pull back to check that she's okay. "Use your colours, Kiera."

"Green." The look in her eyes is pure lust, and she's biting that lip again. I gently pull her lip free of her teeth as she stares at me, her breathing getting heavier. I nibble her lip, and she takes hold of my arms.

I reach for the hem of her t-shirt, yanking it over her head. Her hair falls effortlessly around her shoulders once more. I stand back and admire her body. It is beautiful. Kiera hates the gym, running, and, from what I've gathered, any form of exercise apart from sex. Her body is slim, untoned, and soft. Perfection. She grins wickedly as she unbuttons her jeans and slowly slides them down her legs, stepping out of them and closer to me. She's now only in her underwear and inches in front of me. I'm trying to rein in my control; otherwise, it'll be over in minutes.

I grab her hips, drag her to me and walk over to the bed, where I throw her down. She giggles as she bounces. My smile widens as I feel those butterflies awaken from hearing it. Pulling my shirt over my head, I toss it to the floor with her clothes. I don't think I'll ever tire of her looking at me like she is now. I know I'm attractive, but it's the way she looks at me, her eyes pouring over my body as if she's trying to imprint me in her memory, like I do with her, if I'm being honest.

I move onto the bed and hover over her. Her eyes

are watching my every move. "You ready, missy?" I say in a husky voice. She bites that bottom lip again, and I grin.

Chapter Eighteen

KIERA

I agreed to be his. I feel like this might be happening too soon, but nothing has felt more right than it does now, at this moment. I'm on Ed's bed in my underwear, and I'm anticipating whatever he has in store for me tonight.

"Are you ready, missy?" His voice sends shivers throughout my body, and I am getting more turned on. The glint in his eyes is pure lust and power. The goosebumps show on my body. All I can muster is a nod.

Ed hovers over me, takes my hands and pins them above my head. His lips are on my neck, biting, sucking, making me shudder with excitement. "Don't move those hands," he orders in a tone that makes me want to do as I'm told. He gets off the bed and goes over to a drawer.

"Turn over and get on your knees." He has a belt. A spike of fear runs through me that makes me pool with warmth down there. I have no idea why. I turn over, and Ed grabs my hands, places them in front of me and ties me to his headboard with the belt. My heart is hammering. I'm face down and ass up. I'm both relieved and a little disappointed that this is why he needed the belt.

"Oh, don't worry, missy. There'll be time for that another day." How does he know?

I'm on display for him, and I feel slightly embarrassed. He moves off the bed again, and I hear him make an appreciative sound. "Oh, Kiera, you really are beautiful." I move my head around to see him out of the corner of my eye. He's taking his remaining clothes off and staring at my ass in the air.

Ed sits on the end of the bed with his back to me and then leans back so that his head is beneath me. I wriggle in anticipation, which earns me a smack on my nearly bare backside. I yelp a little, but not with pain. It is the shock and pleasure of it. Gripping my hips, he lowers me down to his face, teasing me with his nose through my underwear. Then he grabs the thin lace of my knickers around my hips and yanks hard with both hands, forcing the delicate material to snap under the pressure. He throws the scraps to the floor.

Well, that's one less pair I have to wash, I chuckle to myself.

His hands roam over my ass and hips, pressing me against his face. His tongue teases me, and I lower myself a little more for the added friction. "Kiera, patience." My breath hitches. He's bossy, and I love it. The teasing soon stops when his tongue circles my clit, making me groan with ecstasy. His fingers stroke my entrance, and before I register what's happening, he thrusts two fingers inside me, making me moan embarrassingly loud. He laughs softly, and the vibrations make my eyes roll back in my head.

I can feel the pressure building as he eats me as if I'm his last meal. "Oh, Ed!" With that as his cue, he bites down on my clit, and I explode into an intense orgasm, my legs trembling as he laps me up.

As I'm coming down, he moves beside me and flips me over with ease. "Good girl," he says as he strokes himself whilst watching me.

I lick my lips. His cock is big, and I want it in my mouth. As if he can read my mind, he's shifted over to the side of my head, eager to please him. Holding onto the headboard and my hair, he guides himself into my mouth with a hiss. I gaze up at him. His eyes are burning into mine with such passion as he pumps himself into my mouth. I gag slightly as he goes deeper, but I don't pull back. Something inside me wants to be his good girl. With that thought, I flush and get wetter.

Ed's grunting stops as he pulls himself out of my mouth. "Damn, Kiera, I nearly blew there. Your mouth is so fuckable." He winks and leans down to kiss me hard. His fingers tease my nipples one at a time before he slides between my legs, which shamelessly fall wide open for him. He eases me onto my side and into position. My hands are still bound, and I have one leg underneath him, and another raised just above his hips as he teases my entrance before thrusting into me hard.

"Jesus!" I can't help but shout. This is a position

I've never been in, but my God, it's hitting all the right places. Ed shifts my legs, wrapping them around his hip and uses one hand to tease my clit as the other teases my ass. My eyes roll back into my head again as I come over and over whilst he thrusts into me at a punishing rate. He dips his thumb deeper into my ass and drives harder into me, making me explode around him one last time before he finds his own release.

I'm spent. Completely and utterly spent.

He laughs softly as he kisses me, releasing my hands from their restraint, and I flop onto my back. He moves beside me, wraps us both in the duvet and inspects my wrists. I tell him they don't feel sore, which they don't. Ed rests his head on his hand as he strokes my belly with the other underneath the duvet. We lay there in comfortable, sated silence. I can hear Ed asking if I'm feeling okay and grabbing water from the bedside table. The next moment, he lifts my head slightly so I can drink some before he rubs my arms, which feels nice after having them tied for a while.

When I've finally come back down to earth, I sit up gingerly because my entire body aches in such a wonderful way, and I suddenly need to pee.

Chapter Nineteen

ED

We pull up at my parent's house, and I'm nervous. Kiera grabs my hand as we walk in. She has a fierce look on her face, and I feel a little better knowing I have her by my side.

"We've got this," she says as she squeezes my hand.

It's been an hour since we've arrived. My mum naturally loves Kiera. I mean, what's not to love? My dad, a quiet character, has been laughing at her jokes. She really is the light in a world that has many dark places. My brother isn't here yet, and according to my parents, he might not come.

"So, Kiera, please tell us how you managed to get this one off the market? He's not one for relationships, you know." Mum is relaxed and is looking at Kiera with genuine interest. She probably doesn't mean to sound condescending, but some of her comments have that edge. It might be my imagination after the years of abuse, but when I notice Kiera's back straighten a little more, I realise she takes it that way, too.

"Well, Mrs Green, we're the perfect fit for each other. I have been on *the market* for a while, and it wasn't until I met Ed that things fit into place," Kiera responds, wiggling her fingers in the air with the "on the market" quote.

My dad is grinning behind my mum. He's a strong man, tall, broad and wise, but when it comes to my mum, he hovers in the background and leaves her to fill the space. She's a little smaller than him in stature, but her character is as strong as he is quiet. She has always been the talker, the social butterfly who won't let anyone get a word in edgewise. My mum is wearing an expression that is a mix of amusement and pride, offering a bemused smile whilst there is a little gleam in her eyes.

"Ed, you've got yourself a live one here. Well done, my boy." Mum smiles at me. She pulls me into a hug and gives me a kiss on the cheek. Mum was always lovely when I was growing up, but always took my brother's side. He was her first baby, after all. I'm still convinced she knew at least some of what happened but chose to live in ignorant bliss rather than deal with it.

I kiss Kiera's hand and go to the kitchen to grab us another drink, and then I hear his voice. My body freezes, my hands shake, and I can't move. As humans, we have a flight or fight response. There is a third response, freeze, which seems to be what I do whenever I am near Noel. He's not in the house, but I can hear him in the garden. I turn to see him beeline for Kiera. I take a minute to compose myself before returning to her. If he thinks he can stake a claim on what's mine, he's got another thing coming—no matter how scared I still am of him.

I walk over to Kiera and Noel, pushing down my fear and replacing it with fake confidence. He bends down to talk to her quietly, but she says something that makes him both glare at her and look petrified at the same time. Kiera smiles smugly and has a little bit of an evil glint in her eyes. I'm suddenly really turned on.

As I reach them, I hand Kiera her drink and kiss her forehead. "Hey, baby," I say with a calm smile, even though my palms are sweating. "Noel." I nod to him.

"Ed." His voice is barbed, and there's a look in his eyes that has me cowering in the corner of my mind.

"Ed, Noel was just telling me about how well he's doing in his new job. Apparently, he's going up for a promotion soon." She smirks at me. I need to find out what she said to him that's making her look mischievous.

"Well, yeah, I'm the best salesman there is in the garage. They'd be stupid not to promote me to senior sales. I can get any car I want, baby." He winks at her.

"I'm sure that line will be fine for the level of woman you normally attract, but for someone of my calibre, you need to offer much more. Like your brother here." She winks at me, and I stand a little taller. "Now, if you'll excuse me, gentleman, I need to go to the ladies." She stretches up on her toes and kisses me passionately. As much as I absolutely love this, I think she's making a point, and when I glance at my brother, I think the point was driven home. He looks embarrassed and a little smaller than a few minutes ago.

"How on earth did a shit like you manage to pull someone like that? You must be paying her," Noel sneers. My mind is telling me to run to my room and hide. This is the same tone of voice that normally came before the beatings. But I can't. I'm older now. I'm stronger physically, and I'm really trying mentally. He can't win if I don't let him anymore.

"Ha! Is that how you get your girls?" I regret my remark immediately when his expression morphs into anger, and I see that look in his eyes. He wants to hurt me.

Kiera comes bounding back, her lightness scaring away the dark he's forcing around me. "Noel, I suggest you go and rescue your Bambi over there. She's not moved in over twenty minutes, and you haven't been very gentlemanly and offered her a drink yet, have you?" Kiera shifts her gaze to a woman who appears petrified to be here but is staying where he left her. I didn't even notice he came with someone, but Kiera did. I study the other woman more closely. Her arms are crossed, hugging her body, and her eyes are darting around, but she keeps checking the spot where Noel is. Is he hurting other people?

Noel says nothing and storms over to the poor girl, whose eyes widen as he approaches. He grabs her elbow and drags her into the house.

"Your brother is a piece of shit. If this wasn't my first time meeting your parents, I'd happily put him in his place."

"Well, you said something that upset him earlier. What was it?" I turn to stare at her, genuinely curious.

"I told him I knew all his dirty little secrets, and if he lays a hand on me again, I will shout them for the world to hear, and then his lovely parents will no longer have a choice to ignore it." She holds her head high, her lips twitching into a self-assured smile.

I smile and kiss her. This woman is remarkable.

I have a feeling inside me that I haven't had in a long time. Warmth.

Chapter Twenty

It's getting late, and I want to go home soon. It's been a lovely afternoon at Ed's parent's house. I've met some nice people...except for his dickhead brother. That man has me wanting to learn how to torture people. I'm chatting with Ed's mum, and I catch Ed looking at me. He has a beautiful smile.

I excuse myself and walk over to him. "I'm going to go to the loo, and then shall we go? I've got a lot on tomorrow."

"Absolutely, love. I'll go and tell my parents we're leaving soon." He smiles after me as I enter the house.

The downstairs loo is occupied, so I head upstairs. There's no way I can wait any longer. I drink when I'm nervous, no matter the liquid, and I drank a lot today. Luckily, it was mainly soft drinks, meaning I won't be hungover tomorrow. The upstairs bathroom of Ed's family home is lovely and traditional, and I'm thankful to have a couple of minutes to myself. I forgot how draining meeting new people can be, but I'm here for Ed.

As I sit, having a look round the bathroom, I hear floorboards creaking, and although there are a lot of people about, I'm suddenly on edge. I finish up in the bathroom and walk out to find Ed, but I'm slammed against a wall, and the wind is knocked out of me.

"You little slut. You think you can get away with threatening me?" Noel is a dick, but I totally understand why Ed has been terrified of him. There's something in his eyes that tells me he could kill me. That's not normal.

"Get your hands off me," I say loudly in the hope someone will hear me, but the house sounds quiet. My fear is heightened, but I'm trying to not let it show as Noel moves closer to me. His hands are running down my body, and his face is in my hair, sniffing the crook of my neck. I can feel bile rising in my throat, but I push it down the best I can. Noel has me pinned to the wall with his body, and I can feel him getting turned on by this, which is making the bile rise again. I'm trying to wriggle away from him, and he mutters "slut" and "whore" before pinning my arms behind my back with one hand and wrapping my hair round his other hand, forcing my neck to tilt up.

He licks my neck, and I can't even muster the voice to shout. That's when I hear faint footsteps. Noel hasn't appeared to have heard them yet.

"Get your fucking hands off my girl." Ed's voice is deep and controlled and has Noel moving away from me slightly, but he still has me half-pinned. "I said, get your FUCKING hands off my girl." I can see the anger in Ed's eyes now. I'm trying my hardest to stop the tears that are threatening to fall.

"Oh, I heard you. I just don't know who gave you the balls to talk to me like that. You know what happens when you try to run. I will do what I did to you all those years ago. I will find you, beat you and make you feel pain like you have never felt before. You are pathetic, weak and don't deserve an ounce of love."

"You are the one who's pathetic, Noel. You had to beat your own brother for what? Love from your parents? Were you worried he was better than you? You should have been. He's a thousand times the man you will ever be. And to call me a whore? Is that the only way you can get women to hang out with you? Because your personality is worse than a cockroach with chlamydia. No one wants you." My anger is rising to a dangerous level, which is soon calmed by Ed laughing so hard he nearly falls over.

Noel stares between us. We may not have been able to handle him individually when we were caught off guard, but together, we are a formidable team. Stepping away from me, Noel slaps me across the face, knocking me to the floor. Damn! That is painful. I glare at him with my tear-filled eyes as Ed balls his fists and stalks towards his brother.

Just as Ed is about to swing at Noel, a bellow comes from the stairs, "ENOUGH!"

Ed's dad, Henry, stomps up the stairs. "Kiera, love,

please go and see Angela in the kitchen and get that seen to. I'll take it from here." As I move towards Ed, Henry places a hand on my shoulder and squeezes slightly. I don't know what is going to happen, but I'm glad to be leaving. I just wish I could take Ed with me.

Chapter Twenty-One

ED

The years of anger, shame and resentment have all come to the surface. I'm ready to kick the living shit out of Noel. Then, out of nowhere, my dad shouts. I've never heard him raise his voice before. I have no idea what to do in this situation. My mum was the disciplinarian in our family. She raised her voice occasionally, but my dad didn't. I stand there staring at him, but then get a little of that anger back when I remember he was about to stop me from punching my vile brother. I swear, I'll walk away from this family if I get any of the blame for this.

Noel looks just as stumped as I do but quickly plays the victim. He furrows his brows, and…has that fucker started to tear up on demand? He's an actual psychopath! "Dad—" he begins, but my father holds his hand up to silence him.

"For years, I didn't see what was under my nose. I didn't even think to question if there was anything wrong. You were a happy little boy until your brother came along." He shakes his head and glances down at the floor for a moment. Raising his gaze again, he stares at Noel and continues, "Was it jealousy? Your mum and I loved you both the same. Didn't you learn that every time Ed had another *accident*, he ended up getting a little more attention? We honestly thought he was *that* clumsy. And even when Ed left home at seventeen, I thought, 'It's too early, but he's determined to be independent.' Now I see that he was running from you."

"Dad, no, you have it all wrong," Noel pleads, but my dad's body is rigid, his legs planted in a wide stance, his hands are shaking whilst he's flexing his fingers, and his eyes are bulging with anger.

"Then you come into my house, make fun of Ed all afternoon, and disgustingly hit his girlfriend. I have NEVER been so ashamed as I am right now." My dad is shaking, but I think it's mostly anger at this point. He turns to me; I cower a little, not knowing what to expect as I've never seen this side of him before. He walks over to me and wraps me in his arms. "I'm sorry, Ed. I should have protected you, and I didn't. I'm proud of the man you are, and that firecracker you have downstairs is a keeper," he says quietly. I hug him back; I can't remember the last time I felt this amount of love from him.

Noel pushes past us to walk downstairs, and my dad straightens. "Noel, did I say we were finished? Ed, go downstairs to your mum and Kiera. I'll catch up with you later." I brush past Noel with my head held high, exuding confidence I'd faked around him until now. He does nothing but glare at me.

"Angela, really, I'm okay," I hear Kiera say to my mum as I walk into the kitchen. I look at Mum, and tears are running down her face.

"Mum?"

She peers up at me, and loud sobs escape her as she rushes to hug me. "I'm so sorry. I'm sorry, Ed. Please forgive me. I'm sorry." She shakes in my arms. I'm a little taller than my mum, so her head is resting on my shoulder whilst she sobs.

"Shhh. Mum, it's okay. I'm putting it behind me where it belongs."

I look at Kiera, who's watching this emotional moment. I wanted her with me today so I didn't feel scared. Instead, she got hurt. The amount of guilt that washes over me when I see her red cheek turning purple is unreal. I mouth, "I'm so sorry," to her, but she cocks her head and gives me a small smile, making her wince with pain.

I push my mum away from my shoulder and study her. She looks broken. "Mum, what happened years ago was awful. It is something that still affects me to this day, but I'm getting better now. I couldn't tell you. He got into my head, telling me you wouldn't believe me. I wanted to on a couple of occasions, and I think he saw that, and I stopped wanting to try when Noel said he'd kill me. I believed him. I hoped you'd notice, but he was and still is a good actor. I remember the doctors asking me a few times if I was being abused, but they tried to blame you and Dad, not Noel. I kept with the same story. It was an accident. I fell." She sobs quietly as she listens. "I love you, Mum." She flings herself into me, hugging me tighter than I ever knew she had the strength to do.

Mum places her hand on my cheek, and a fresh set of tears stream down her face. "My boy…"

"Mum, I'm okay. Kiera was a right 'firecracker', as Dad calls her."

This makes Mum smile and jolt as if she suddenly remembers she was tending to a bruised and swollen face before I came down. Mum scurries back to Kiera.

I walk over and kiss Kiera on the forehead. "I'm so sorry you got caught up in this. I didn't think he'd touch you. I shouldn't have been surprised after seeing the girl he came with, but it still did. That reminds me, where is she?"

We all look at each other and grow concerned. We saw him walk into the house with her but didn't see her come out. We search for a good ten minutes on the ground floor until I hear a noise under the stairs. I open the cupboard door and see her curled up in a ball with a black eye, crying silently. This poor woman. I crouch down but don't move closer. "Hey, it's okay." I offer my hand to help her up, but her eyes widen, and I think they may fall out of her head. "What's your name?"

"Steph," She says quietly, and I can barely hear her. Noel has really done a number on her. I call out to Mum and Kiera, who come over to help Steph into the kitchen.

Steph follows them cautiously with her head down.

Kiera and Mum's reactions when they see her in proper light are polar opposites. Mum cries, covering her face, and Kiera balls her fists, looking as if she's about to murder Noel.

They sit Steph down next to Kiera, who helps with her bruises, whilst Mum makes her a cup of tea. Finally, Steph opens up about how she met Noel.

She's a single mum struggling for cash, so her friend recommended becoming an escort. There's no sex involved. So she thought, why not? It'd help her provide for her son. She'd been hired by Noel a few times to attend different events, but the last time she messed up and laughed at his colleague's joke at a work event. He didn't like it and took her home and beat her.

When he requested her again, she was nervous but needed the cash and went along. This time was much worse. He forced her to have sex with him. She cried and lashed out the whole time. He hit her so hard that she passed out. He requested her a few times after that, and the same thing happened. Each time, he got more violent. Today was her last job as an escort. She couldn't risk being killed and leaving her boy an orphan.

I look at Kiera whilst Steph talks, and she has tears in her eyes and anger in those balled-up fists.

Chapter Twenty-Two

KIERA

Steph is telling us about her life. Her husband died in a motorbike accident before the baby was born, leaving her and her son alone. She works two jobs and takes care of him. The escort job is a top-up for cash flow. She's barely meeting her bills. I feel sorry for her, and then to be beaten for by that utter piece of filth…

She came here today, and since it was a family event, she thought she'd be safe. I grab her hand as she speaks, and she flinches away before apologising. "Steph, please do not apologise. Everything you've been through…" I can't finish the sentence, but I squeeze her hand.

Steph is telling us about her son, Michael, who is an energetic and smart five-year-old when Henry appears in the kitchen. He takes one look at Steph and curses out loud. "Angela, dear, we need to talk," Henry says bleakly. They disappear into the living room whilst

Ed and I make sure Steph is okay and isn't hurt badly enough to need a hospital.

After half an hour, Angela and Henry come back into the kitchen. Angela's eyes are redder and puffier than before they left us. She looks subdued compared to the women I met hours earlier. Henry makes his apologies and steps back into the living room to make a call. Angela sits down, and I make her a latte using their coffee machine and put a drop of Irish whiskey in to calm her.

She smiles up at me. "You are such a good girl."

Ed goes over to his mum and hugs her tightly. Henry comes back into the kitchen, and I wonder where Noel is. I haven't seen him since he was upstairs.

"Right, then, I've had a serious chat with Noel. He's secured in his bedroom, and the police are on their way with a mental health crisis team. With any luck, he'll be taken to a psychiatric hospital to get help with his violent behaviour." He looks a little troubled before he continues, a deep frown furrowing his brow. "He has severe issues that need to be dealt with so this…" Henry chokes back a sob, and tears are in his eyes, "so this is the only way I can stop him from hurting anyone else. Ed, I cannot apologise enough for not seeing this earlier. Kiera, I'm so sorry for what you had to go through today. And you, young lady, I…" Henry's tears are flowing down his cheeks.

Steph hugs him. "You don't have to apologise. I got myself into this mess." She hugs him again as if his life depended on it, and Henry wraps his arms around her.

"No, love, you didn't. I'm sorry."

We spend another couple of hours at Ed's parents' house. During this time, the police attend and take statements. Noel has been taken to the hospital for further assessment of his mental health whilst in police custody. Steph is being given a lift home by Henry. Ed and I make our way back to his. He is adamant I stay at his this evening, so we pop back to mine to quickly grab my work stuff and some clothes.

We are sitting on his sofa, and he is stroking my face. "Kiera, I'm sorry you got hurt, but I'm also thankful you were with me today. Who knows how long he would have continued to hurt other people. I'm regretful you were one of them." He kisses me softly, and after, I lay my head on his lap, and he strokes my hair, watching whatever film he's put on the TV.

I don't realise I've fallen asleep until I'm being laid down in his bed. My eyes are closed, and I can't open them, but I feel Ed taking off my clothes and putting the duvet over me. There's a dip in the bed, telling me he's joined me, and he wraps his arm over me. I drift back off to sleep, feeling safe and happy.

———

It's been three weeks since the debacle at Ed's parents. My bruise took a couple of weeks to fade, so I've been working from either home or Ed's office. I didn't want to answer any awkward questions in the office. I'm on a video call with my manager. Although she knew roughly what happened and was happy for me to stay at home until my face healed, she's getting quite frustrated that I haven't been in the office, especially when I have a huge contract to deal with.

I finish up the call and head over to the fridge for a snack. I'm working at mine today since Ed went into the office. It feels strange to be apart. We've seen each other daily since we got together. I wonder if this is what Jess felt like with Gavin when they started out?

I grab myself a chocolate bar and go about finishing up some admin work. I will be back in the office tomorrow and want to be ahead. Whilst I'm looking forward to going back in, I do enjoy working from home. It's quiet here.

I think about the drama from a few weeks ago. What would have happened if I wasn't there? Would Noel have continued beating Steph? Would he have continued his reign of terror over Ed? His parents are distraught.

Noel has recently been committed to a psychiatric hospital whilst awaiting trial. He's being charged for his crimes, and no one has heard from him since. He's in intensive therapy for the first few months, and then he'll be allowed contact with the outside world. I feel a little deflated thinking about him. My hand goes to my cheek whilst I'm deep in thought. I've never been smacked across the face before. That really hurt.

I think about Angela and Henry and how they have been with Ed since that weekend. He would normally speak to them once a month and see them every few, but they've been calling daily. The guilt they are carrying is weighing heavily on them. They want to show him he's loved and that they're sorry they never saw it. Ed is frustrated. He's been on his own since he was seventeen, and he survived, but I have told him that having a better relationship with his parents, especially one where they are more honest with each other, is not a bad thing.

I finish up my work and decide to have a nice soak in the bath. I'm usually a shower girl, but sometimes my mind and body need to relax in nice smelling water that is hotter than the centre of the earth.

Chapter Twenty-Three

ED

F our weeks after the shit show at Mum and Dad's party, my feet pound the pavement as I run harder and faster. Since being with Kiera, I have not run as much, but I need this right now. This is my stress relief. It is freedom.

For years, I've been on my own. Years! And suddenly, my parents are back in my life, wanting to know every detail. It's not that they weren't in my life before; they were, but not this close. I've always kept them at arm's length because I always thought they knew what happened and allowed it to happen. Is this what a normal relationship with your parents is like? Constantly talking, them wanting to know what you had for dinner or what your plans are? I run faster. I can't cope with this.

Aching and sweaty, I return to my apartment. I pop my head into the bedroom to see Kiera still snoring away and breathe easier. I instantly feel happier when

I'm with her. The butterflies have calmed, but every now and then, I simply have to look at her, and the tornado they cause in my stomach starts again.

I stand in the shower facing the wall, hot water running down my body, washing the thoughts away. I jump when I feel Kiera's hand on me. Well, it better be her; otherwise, I'm about to get murdered whilst I'm naked.

I turn around to see her freshly woken face. She's utterly adorable in the mornings. She stretches up to kiss me, and I drag her body closer to mine. I'm instantly aroused by her.

My need for her rises as I push her back against the tiles. She gasps as the coldness of the wall hits her back. "This is going to be quick and rough," I warn her as I lift her to wrap her legs around my waist. I ease my tip into her and thrust hard. Damn, she feels good. I grab her shoulders and slam her down onto me with each thrust. She's trembling around me in no time. I love that Kiera likes it rough, too. Within minutes, I've found my release and am leaning heavily against her to catch my breath.

I lower her again, and Kiera places her hands on either side of my face and kisses me before she washes me silently. How did I find this one? She somehow knows I need this. I was desperate for a release and closeness, and now, I'm staring at her. The butterflies are swirling around. I think I'm falling in love. I meant what I said to her. She's mine, and there's no way I'm ever letting her go.

I'M WALKING HOME FROM THE STATION LATE, LISTENING to a podcast with my earphones. Kiera is out with her workmates tonight, and I'm going to eat my burrito and chill until she comes home tipsy and horny. One of my favourite mixes. I am a little on edge. I've been working through my anger over the last few months with my counsellor and am feeling better, but since getting off the train, I'm agitated. I wonder if it's because my woman isn't home. That's ridiculous, though.

I grab my keys from my bag, and when I pause the podcast, I see the reflection of someone behind me in the door to my apartment building. I freeze. I know that reflection. He approaches me, and I leave my keys in the bag. There's no way he's getting me inside to isolate me again.

I turn and look at him. The anger and twisted glint he once had in his eyes is still there but much quieter. His face is drawn, and he has dark circles under his eyes. His body, which was once toned, appears smaller in the tracksuit he's wearing, something he wouldn't have been caught dead in before. This man looks smaller than he once did, but my instincts are telling me to keep my guard up.

"What are you doing here?" I demand harshly.

"We need to talk. Can I come in?" His voice is quiet; it doesn't hold the bold confidence it once had.

"Not a chance." I glare at Noel. All I see is the

years of pain he caused. Plus, the way he was with Kiera riles my anger once again.

"Ed, please."

"I said no. There's a café down the street."

We walk down the street in silence. I walk tall with a new confidence I never had around him. Noel slouches with his hands in his pockets. He looks different. But I won't be lulled into a false sense of security. We enter the café and sit near the window. I'm not about to be backed into a corner. I order us coffee and sit with my arms crossed, waiting for him to speak.

A few minutes pass, and his gaze moves from me to the window. Our coffee hits the table, and then he stares at that. "Noel, you said you wanted to talk. I haven't got all night." I think about my burrito getting soggy in my bag, another thing he's ruined. Every minute that passes by, my anger rises. I drink half my coffee before he decides to look me in the eye.

"I'm sorry," he mutters quietly.

"What?"

"For what I did."

"That's it? You're sorry? You're sorry for torturing me from my toddler years to my teen years? You're sorry you broke my bones, confidence and spirit? You're sorry for taking my carefree childhood and turning it into fear, horror and shame?" I have no idea where those words are coming from, but I mean every one of them. I once had a fantasy about telling him exactly this, but I never imagined I would get the chance to actually do it.

Noel drops his gaze to his hands, which are holding

his coffee cup. For as long as I can remember, he has always been ruthless, mean and hard. Now, looking at him, he's pathetic. I know I should feel something; he's my brother, after all, but after years of hell, there's no way I'm going to forgive him easily.

"Look at me." The words come out of my mouth with such venom, even I wince a little. Noel peers up at me. Is he crying? Fuck off.

"Ed…"

I don't want to relax around him; I don't even know how to, but part of me believes he's sorry.

Chapter Twenty-Four

KIERA

I'm drunk and horny. I stagger up to Ed's apartment building. He gave me a key a few weeks ago, so I let myself in, expecting to find him waiting for me. Ed knows how I am when I drink, and he's always happy to oblige. Tonight, though, I walk into a dark flat. Where is he?

"Ed?" I call out, turning on the lights. Something doesn't feel right. I know he was working a little late tonight, but he texted me saying he was off the train and walking home so he could wait for his drunk girlfriend to come and ravage him. It made me giggle, but now, I'm starting to worry.

I pull out my phone. No missed calls or text messages. I call him, but it goes to voicemail. Ed never lets his phone go below fifty per cent, so it shouldn't be a low battery. I open the Find My app. We shared our locations with each other just in case. Next to his name is "No location found." I fidget a little. Maybe he went for a run? I check his wardrobe and find his running shoes. Nope, not that, then.

I make myself a coffee and think about where he could be. We were definitely meant to be staying here tonight and not at mine. I try his phone again. Straight to voicemail. I down my coffee, grab my keys and head out the door. I don't even know where to begin searching, but I'm starting to get worried. I leave the building and decide to walk towards the café. It's somewhere we will occasionally get late-night snacks. Normally, we have them delivered, but it's a start.

As I near the café, I can see him sitting in a window seat. He's not alone. I don't recognise the other person at first, but when Ed spots me walking towards the café, the person he's with looks out the window, too, and I freeze. I don't know what to do or what to feel. I never thought I'd see Ed having a coffee with his brother. Ed speaks to Noel for a moment before stepping outside.

"Hey, beautiful. Sorry, I wasn't home. I won't be long, and then I'll come back." I glance between him and Noel, who is watching our interaction. "It's a long story, but I'm okay."

"I was worried about you. I couldn't get through on the phone."

Ed frowns and pulls his phone from his pocket and rolls his eyes. "I was listening to a podcast and didn't shut my screen off when I paused it. It must have died. I'm sorry to have worried you." He kisses me on the forehead, and I relax a little. He does seem okay.

"I'll go and wait for you like a good girl then." I

wink at him. He grabs my arms and pulls me to him for a passionate kiss.

"I'll be home soon, baby." He returns to the café, and I wander back to his apartment. I'm feeling snacky now that I've smelt the café's food, and I know there are leftovers in his fridge.

I wake up dazed. I don't remember falling asleep, but a rush of pleasure surging through me has me opening my eyes and seeing Ed's head between my legs. My back arches off the bed as he drives two fingers into me, and I can feel him smiling.

"Wakey wakey, sunshine," he says sexily before giving me another orgasm.

Once my body has come down from the euphoric high, he moves up and kisses me, letting me taste myself on him. He's acting incredibly satisfied with himself with his messed up hair and a lopsided grin on his face.

"I didn't realise I'd fallen asleep, but feel free to wake me up like that anytime." I wink at him.

"I was home a little later than I'd planned, but I wanted you, so here we are." He grins wickedly and carefree. I haven't seen him like this in weeks, not since that weekend.

Just as I am about to respond, he flips me over and, without warning, drives straight into me.

"Oh God!" My senses are waking up after my nap.

Ed smacks my ass, which shoots an electric current of pleasure through me. He grabs my hair and pulls me up so my back is against his chest, and his free hand is rolling and pinching my nipples. Before I know it, I can feel the build-up again. Ed can feel it, too, and he growls in my ear, "Hold it."

How am I meant to hold it? My body somehow obeys him as he keeps me constantly on the edge of exploding. He's hard and thick, and at this angle, he's hitting all the right spots. Ed releases my hair and slides his hand around my throat as he increases his speed. I need to come; I can't keep this pressure at bay any longer.

"Ed, please," I whimper, my brain hardly able to comprehend words.

"Nearly there. Don't come. I promise it'll be worth it." His grip around my throat tightens a little more, which sends tingles throughout my body.

"Come for me, Kiera," he growls, and my body explodes into the most intense orgasm I've ever experienced. It rolls over me in waves, and I see bright stars as he thrusts into me a few more times before I feel him come inside me, which sends another wave of pleasure through my body.

Ed chuckles behind me and kisses my neck. "Good girl. You've soaked my bed."

I'm barely able to register my own body at this point, but my knees are feeling a little damp. What the hell is that?

Ed pulls out and lays us both down next to the damp patch. He litters my face and neck with kisses. My body still feels completely disjointed from my brain. We lie there for a few more minutes, catching our breath, and then I roll over and cup Ed's face and kiss him gently. I have no words for what I just experienced.

He chuckles against my lips. "Are you okay there, love?"

I smile as the feeling of my body comes back to me. "God, yes," is all I can manage. Ed pulls me onto him, and I drift off almost immediately. The last thing I feel is Ed's hand running up and down my back and the warmth of his body next to mine.

Chapter Twenty-Five

ED

I lie awake most of last night with Kiera sleeping in my arms. After the chat with Noel, my mind is racing.

At six in the morning, I leave Kiera in bed to go for a run. She's sleeping well after last night. I was inside her when her orgasm exploded through her, and I nearly came as soon as her first orgasm hit because she squeezed me so tightly. I smile to myself with the memory and run harder.

My chat with Noel wasn't expected. I honestly didn't think I'd ever have to see him again. He'd managed to get a weekend pass from the hospital due to his improvement in therapy. He apologised, and not the sorry excuse of an apology I got in front of my apartment. He apologised for everything: the pain, the isolation, the nightmares, and the endless days and nights I was terrified of being alone with him. He seemed genuinely remorseful.

Noel tried to explain that sometimes he felt like he wasn't in control of his own body and that his anger took over. I shake my head as I run. I understand sometimes we do things we don't mean to, but there still needs to be accountability. Which he appears to be accepting now. He told me about the girls he used and abused. Steph wasn't the first, but thankfully, she will be the last. He felt guilty for everything he did to Kiera. He wanted to hurt me, and she was an easier target than getting to me. I didn't know he could feel guilt.

By the time I get back home, Kiera isn't in bed or the shower. Where is she? I check my phone, and I have no messages from her, either. I jump in the shower, and when I step out, she's sitting at the dining table with a coffee and a couple of croissants from the local café. She smiles at me, and my apartment brightens around her. I'm falling in love with her a little more. Not that I can tell her yet. It's too soon.

"Hey there, handsome." She walks over and kisses me. "Want to talk about last night?" Kiera speaks softly with a kind look in her eyes. I sit down and tell her about my conversation with Noel last night. She listens and sips her coffee. I can't not be honest with her, especially after everything we've been through. And I want to be honest with her. She makes me want to be a better version of myself.

I lean back in my chair, watching as Kiera processes everything I tell her. She mirrors my position and asks, "Do you believe him?"

"I think I do. I mean, what else can I do? He

showed more remorse last night than he ever has before, and I can't keep carrying around this shame and anger for the rest of my life."

She nods and finishes the last of her croissant. "Well, if that's what you want to do, babe, and you really feel like you can believe him, then accept his apology and move forward." She smiles sweetly and gets up.

"Come on, let's go for a walk," I say, not wanting to stay cooped up indoors all day. It's too nice out not to enjoy the fresh air.

IN THE LAST WEEK, KIERA AND I HAVE MOVED INTO A new phase of our relationship without really speaking about it. It feels so natural. We've not spent a day apart for months, except when we are in our offices, but then, we're together every evening. I want to ask her to officially move in with me—we practically live together anyway—but is it too soon? She's mine. I want her to move in with me officially.

It's Saturday, and Kiera is away in Paris with her friend Jess for the weekend. I suddenly feel lonely. I miss her. I'm used to having her around, and it feels ridiculous that I can't be home without her here. I give my mum a call. I might pop down for the night, even if it's just for the company.

"Ed love, how are you?" My mum sounds chirpy today. It's an improvement from how she's been since that weekend.

"I'm alright, Mum. Kiera is away this weekend, and I feel a little…"

"Lost?" She chuckles.

"Something like that. Anyway, fancy dinner tonight? I don't fancy eating on my own again."

"Well, we have company this evening, but come on over. You know you're always welcome."

I pack an overnight bag and drive over to my parents' house. I pull up on the drive and notice there's a car I've not seen before. My guard goes up, yet I don't know why. Getting out of the car, I decide to leave my bag behind just in case and walk into the house to the sound of laughter. I hear a child. Who's here?

"Ed dear, is that you?" My mum calls from the kitchen. I move in that direction and struggle to understand what's in front of me. My mum is at the kitchen table with Steph, the woman who was beaten by Noel. There's a child—I'm assuming her son Michael—in the back garden chasing my dad around and giggling. I'm stunned. I wasn't expecting this. Are these the guests who are staying for dinner?

"Hey." I feel like I'm talking in slow motion.

"Ed, you remember Steph?"

Steph swings round and smiles broadly. She looks completely different from when I last saw her. She's fuller, has colour in her face and seems happy. She's beautiful. "Hi." She grins as she jumps up to give me a hug. "Thank you for helping to save me. You're truly a knight in shining armour."

I pat her on the back and step away. As nice as this

is, it feels a little too touchy for my liking. I walk over and give my mum a kiss before heading to the back garden. The kid stops running and stares at my dad.

How much time do they spend together? "It's okay, Michael. This is my youngest son, Ed." I kneel down and smile at the boy. If I remember correctly, I think he's about six. He acts very timid in front of me but appears to be incredibly close with my dad.

I have a lot of questions.

Chapter Twenty-Six

ED

Half an hour later, and we're inside having a cuppa. Mum has been filling me in on the last few weeks whilst Dad has been playing in the living room with Steph and Michael.

"The guilt, Ed. It tore us to pieces. This poor girl was trying to provide for her son and keep a roof over their heads, and what Noel did…" She sniffs, I reach out, putting my hand on hers.

"It's not your fault, Mum."

"I know, dear, but there's no way I could sit back and pretend nothing happened. And when Steph left that night, we exchanged numbers. We met up a couple of times, and I met her boy. He's such a little darlin'. She was struggling because her neighbour, who always looked after Michael for her when she worked, ended up in hospital after breaking her hip. So we offered to babysit." Mum busied herself with making a fresh teapot whilst we spoke. She needed to stay busy, by the looks of it.

"We've gotten close, and we wanted to do more to help. Dad and I paid her rent for the next few months and helped her out with a car so she didn't have to rely on buses." I sit back in shock. Well, I'm not too shocked since my parents will help anyone, but this is big help. I hope Steph isn't taking advantage of their kindness.

"She's not a gold digger. She's a genuine person who's had a bad deck handed to her."

"I just don't want you and Dad to be taken advantage of, Mum. That's all."

Mum shakes her head and comes to sit next to me. "Ed, she's been through so much already. No family, and the only person who was kind to her was her neighbour. We've developed such a wonderful relationship. It's lovely having a little one running around, and it eases our guilt. I know you're protective, but you don't need to be with Steph."

I sit back. She does seem like a nice woman, and her son is absolutely besotted with my dad. I hear squeals of excitement coming from the living room. As my mum potters around the kitchen, I go see what is happening. Steph has tears in her eyes, and Michael can barely contain his excitement. Dad got him one of those big Lego boxes with lots of different things to build. Standing there, I smile at them. Michael's happy mood is infectious. I'm starting to understand why Mum and Dad love having them around.

"Thank you, Henry. Can we open it now?"

Michael is literally bouncing where he sits on the floor next to Dad.

"It's up to your mum." Dad grins at Steph who has a lone tear rolling down her cheek.

"Of course, darling. Henry, you really didn't have to. You've already done so much for us."

Dad waves his hand at her and goes about opening the Legos with Michael. I can't tell who is more excited.

Steph stands and pauses when she sees me. "I didn't ask. Honestly. It was a surprise to me, too."

I can tell she is nervous. I only know a small portion of what this woman had been through, but this seems to be a welcomed break for her. "Steph, don't worry. Mum and Dad love spoiling people. Let them." I smile and gesture for her to follow me. We walk out into the garden and sit on the bench in silence for a few minutes.

"I'm sorry for what he did to you." I don't look at her when I say this, but I want her to know.

"Your mum told me about you. I'm sorry he did that to you, too." We sit, looking over the garden, listening to the birds sing their songs and to Michael's excitement coming from inside. She smiles when she hears her son's happiness.

"How long have you been on your own?"

"Since Michael was a baby. My husband died in an accident. It's just been me and Michael since." Steph sighs, sadness emanating from her.

"You've done a great job with him. From what I've seen, he's a happy, healthy and lovely kid."

"Thank you, Ed." She smiles with tears in her eyes again. I can't imagine the life she's had, but I know that it's going to be brighter now. Mum and Dad aren't letting her or Michael go anytime soon.

———

MUM HAS COOKED A BEAUTIFUL MEXICAN FEAST tonight. Michael has never tried Mexican food before, and I've never seen anyone so small eat so much. He absolutely loves it. Steph and Michael leave about an hour after dinner, him carrying his new Legos out with a beaming smile on his face.

I'm sitting and looking at my phone. I haven't heard from Kiera today. I know there's only an hour's time difference, but I miss her. I fire off a quick text.

> Me: Hope you're having fun with Jess. Missing you xx

I see those three little dots appear…

> Kiera: Sorry I've not been in touch. Paris is amazing, and we've been shopping all day! Just going out to dinner. Can't wait to see you tomorrow. Missing you too xx

I smile at my phone like a lovestruck teenager. I'm in trouble. I've fallen hard for someone who bumped into me at a bar.

Chapter Twenty-Seven

KIERA

We landed in London a few hours ago. Flying on Gavin's company jet was a luxurious experience I didn't anticipate having. Also, having a lovely weekend away in Paris with my best friend was amazing. I'd love to go there with Ed one day, but I feel as if it is too early to suggest a romantic weekend away. We've become comfortable with each other, and this is the longest we've spent apart since he declared me *his*.

Walking into my flat, it feels strange and empty because I haven't spent much time here lately. We sometimes sleep over at mine, but Ed's place is roomier and has more light. When Ed texted me last night telling me he was missing me, it made my heart loop around in my chest. I missed him, too; I told Jess I think I'm falling for him. We haven't known each other long, but like she said, she and Gavin were a whirlwind romance. They fell hard and fast. Maybe this is what it feels like for some people—overwhelming feelings from the beginning.

It's the middle of the afternoon, and I've put my washing on and started to put the clothes from my shopping spree away. Ed told me he went to his parents' last night, so I'm not sure what time he'll be back. As I'm wrestling the clothes into my wardrobe, my door buzzer sounds.

"Hello?"

"Hey, beautiful." My stomach has butterflies. Oh, how I've missed his voice. I press the door release and go back to trying to close my wardrobe door. I'm nearly there when I feel Ed's arms wrap around my waist. I turn to face him, and he plants a soft kiss on my lips.

"It's ridiculous how much I missed you this weekend," he mumbles against my neck.

I grin. "Just so happens, I missed you, too." I pull his face to mine, and our lips meet again, slowly at first, becoming more needy and passionate as we kiss.

He spins us around and throws me onto my bed. Bouncing, I giggle. Ed is on top of me within seconds. Different from our gentle touching by the wardrobe, his movements are almost desperate. His hands are moving my clothes to touch my skin, and I decide to help the poor man out and take off my top. Ed leans back on his knees and rushes to do the same before his mouth is covering every inch of my exposed skin. I feel like I'm on fire. His teeth tease my nipples through my bra, sending electric currents through my body.

My back arches off the bed with the sensations, and he chooses this time to remove my jeans. It's only been a couple of days since we last saw each other. I missed him, but my body has been missing him as well. Trailing kisses over every inch of my skin, he leaves me breathless, and each one makes me tingle. He rips my thong off, and it's now a useless scrap of material lying on the floor whilst he drives two fingers straight into me. I grasp the covers on the bed as he pushes my bra up with his spare hand and flicks his tongue over my nipples.

"You're so ready for me," he growls as he takes his fingers out and tastes them. Undoing his own jeans, he steadies himself at my entrance and pushes straight into me, making me scream with pleasure and stretching me. I'm building up rapidly when he leans into down next to my ear and says in a voice that thunders, "You're mine. Now, come." And as if my body is under his command, I come with a blinding force.

I'm reeling after that orgasm, but Ed isn't done. He hooks his arms under my knees and pushes deeper into me. The angle has made my eyes roll back into my head. I feel like I'm floating, and out of nowhere, another orgasm comes crashing through my body. I can feel Ed twitching inside me. The deep noises coming from his body are animalistic as he thrusts into me a few more times before throwing his head back, and my name rumbles out of him as he comes.

We collapse in a tangled mess on the bed, panting heavily. When our breathing calms down to a normal level, Ed shifts his body to face me. Looking into my eyes, he utters four words that leave me frozen. "Move in with me."

I lay there like a deer in the headlights. I honestly don't know what to say. Yes, we've been together constantly over the last few months, and this weekend was the longest we've been apart since we got together, but moving in with him seems like a huge step to take. Am I being rational, or am I afraid? I feel like I'm in my head for ages, but in reality, it must only be a few minutes. Ed readjusts himself, propping himself up on his elbow, his other hand cupping my face.

"Kiera, this weekend was torture not being able to be around you. I missed you more than I want to admit. I never thought I'd get to the point I wanted to spend all my time with someone, yet you came into my life and turned it upside down. I want to wake up next to you every day. Move in with me?"

I sit up a little. My brain seems to have stopped thinking other than one question…is it too soon?

Ed must see the thoughts running through my mind because he says, "Take your time. There's a lot to think about. But you will still have your own space, and I'm honestly not scared of any crazy that may come out of you during your period. You've seen a little of my darkness. I'm sure I can handle yours, too."

I roll onto my back and laugh. "Ed, are you sure this isn't too fast?"

"I don't, but then I'm madly in love with you, so I'm biased."

I sit up quickly and almost make myself dizzy. Did he say he's in love with me? I know I am in love with him, but it's magical hearing him say it. I launch myself at him, kissing him frantically.

He loves me!

Chapter Twenty-Eight

ED

W hen my gorgeous woman tears herself off me, her expression will stay with me forever: The relaxed and sated curve to her lips, the pink glow to her cheeks and the way her eyes sparkle with joy. She is full of love, happiness, excitement and comfort.

"I love you, too," she says quietly. "I'll move in with you." Happiness overwhelms me, and I grab her by the waist and pin her beneath me, showering her with kisses.

Smiling, I look down at her, and my heart swells in my chest. I do love this woman. It slipped out earlier, but I'm glad it did. "I'll arrange movers when you're ready."

THE LAST FOUR WEEKS HAVE FLOWN BY. KIERA MOVED in last week. Her flat didn't look like it contained a lot, but it was clearly a Tardis! There are still boxes labelled "stuff" in the office waiting to be unpacked. It's only been a week, but they are making me twitch. When I moved into this apartment, I was unpacked and organised within twelve hours.

I'm reorganising the office space to make room for a desk that's being delivered later today for Kiera. I've also put up some shelves on her side of the office for her books and stuff. Kiera is filling the wardrobe in the bedroom with three more boxes to unpack, mind you, when I hear a bang.

Going to see what the noise was, I find Kiera on the floor with the front of a drawer in her hand and a bewildered expression. "And what have you done now, Missy?" I laugh, taking in the sight. The drawer is over-packed, and something got stuck in the runners, which is why the front came off.

"I have no idea. Your furniture has attitude," she says, frowning, which makes me laugh again.

"If you didn't over-pack it, it might have been alright. You are aware there is a whole other set of drawers for you to use?"

Kiera stares at me and deadpans, "Yeah, that's full."

I honestly have no idea why someone needs so many clothes, but we'll find space. I go online and order two new drawer units and another wardrobe. Luckily, I, or rather we, have the space.

"Lunchtime. I'm starving," I say, pulling her up and kissing the top of her head.

After lunch, we tackle some of the boxes that can be unpacked before the extra furniture arrives to contain the rest of her clothes and stuff.

As the seasons change, we become almost inseparable. Our flat has become *our* home, and our belongings have merged seamlessly—after the original furniture malfunction, of course. It suddenly occurs to me that we've been together for almost a year now, and neither of us has celebrated our birthdays. Mine is next week, and I have no idea when hers is.

I find Kiera moving stuff around on her desk in the office, and I lean against the door frame, taking her in. It's October, but she's wearing a tank top and shorts and is barefoot. As if she can feel my stare, Kiera spins and flashes the widest of smiles that make her eyes crinkle in the corners.

"It's just occurred to me that we've been together nearly a year."

Kiera cocks her head at me as I speak. "Yeah?" she says.

"When's your birthday? We haven't celebrated it yet."

"It's next week. When's yours then?"

"Next week." We both look at each other. "I'm the tenth," I say, surprised that our birthdays are the same week.

"Fifteenth. Looks like we're having a joint celebration." The twinkle in her eye tells me she isn't thinking about a meal out together.

A smile slowly spreads across my face because I know full well what I'm giving her for her birthday, and it isn't something I can buy in the shops. With that thought in mind, my cock twitches with excitement. There may have to be a prequel to the main event. As I cross the room, closing the distance between us in a few strides, Kiera backs up against her desk to perch her perfect arse on the edge.

I grab the back of her neck and kiss her like it's the last one I'll ever get. The sudden need to be inside her is overwhelming. I lift her, pushing her further onto her desk, and she wraps her legs around my waist as she deepens the kiss. I pull at her bottom lip with my teeth, which makes her moan. The beast inside me has woken, and I fist her hair in my hand and wrench back her head, giving me full access to her slender neck. I bite down hard on that sweet spot between her neck and shoulder. The gasp that leaves her mouth has my cock straining in my jeans.

Trailing kisses and nibbles down to her breasts, I yank down her tank top to release her pebbled nipples to lick and bite my way across each of them.

"Ed." Kiera is breathless. In a rush, I pick her up and carry her to the bedroom. My lips and hands do not leave her body until she screams my name four times, and only then do I make her scream it twice more with my cock pounding into her.

As I come down from my euphoric state, I hear Kiera's breathing level out into soft snores beside me.

How did I get so lucky? I wasn't sure a relationship would work, but this woman makes me happy. She made me fall in love with her. If anything were to break this, I have a feeling I would break as well. She has become my life.

Chapter Twenty-Nine

KIERA

Ed and I celebrate our birthdays with small gifts and a lot of hot sex. I bought him a photo cube for his desk that is filled with pictures of me pulling silly faces, and he bought me a pair of beautiful earrings.

After being in the office in back-to-back meetings all day, I am ready for a drink tonight. I message Jess and Ed to see if they're free to join Sarah, Jake and me later. Sarah and Jake have stopped pretending and have become the cutest couple. I don't mind being their third wheel, but it'd be nice to have some extra company.

We head to the pub after work. Jake orders the first round whilst Sarah and I catch up. Since Ed and I have been together, I feel like I've lost touch with some of the people around me. He seems to have become the beginning and end of everything. When Jake arrives back at our table, I check my phone to see if Jess or Ed have messaged me back. Nothing.

The three of us sit and chat for what feels like half an hour, but three hours have flown by. We've drunk too much for a school night and are on our way out. They head off to one station together, and I pop my headphones in and head over to mine. I'm a little concerned that I haven't heard from Ed. He normally responds instantly. Jess, on the other hand, I'm used to her belated replies. She's been like this since way before Gavin. Sometimes, she responds immediately, and other times, I wait three to five business days. I chuckle to myself, thinking about my best friend. I make a mental note to arrange a girl's night soon.

Jumping off at my stop, I wander home, listening to my playlist. Not many people understand my playlists. It goes from 90's pop like Westlife to 80's rock like AC/DC and Metallica, and throw some Ibiza classics in there with Taylor Swift, Michael Bublé and Rob Zombie, and that's the random mix I love listening to. I'm dancing my way down the quiet street to our apartment, listening to a new David Guetta song.

When I walk into our home, I see a glow coming from our bedroom. I remove my air pods and check my phone to see zero notifications from Ed. I haven't heard from him since lunchtime, and although something very simple like his phone dying has happened before, this isn't like him. But as I set my stuff down, thinking that I probably need a snack before bed, I hear shuffling from our room, and I can't wait to playfully lay into Ed about not messaging me back. I stumble quietly towards it, still feeling a little tipsy.

I walk into our room, and the first thing my eyes land on is underwear on the bed. It's not mine, and it looks brand new. It's an understated, sexy set, a deep purple lacy bra with swirl details on the cups and silk straps. It has a matching thong. Not something Ed would normally buy me. He likes bold contrasts such as black and red, although he prefers me in nothing at all.

When I tear my eyes from the underwear, I notice a set of handcuffs on the edge of the bed. Ed has been showing me more of the bondage he likes to use in the bedroom, but all of his restraints are silk or leather with lined cuffs. He's never used metal on me once since it's too quick to cause bruising. I wonder if we're kicking things up a notch, but something very strong inside me tells me this isn't him.

My phone rings in my hand, and at the same time, the hairs on the back of my neck start to prickle, making me jump. It's Jess. I answer, bringing it up to my ear, and I feel someone breathing down the back of my neck.

"Be a good girl, don't say a word and hang up."

Startled, I drop the phone. I freeze in place as he bends down to hang it up, and I can hear Jess saying my name over and over before he grabs me by the shoulders and turns me slowly to face him.

I will not shake. I will not show fear. My body betrays me as it trembles at the sight of his soulless eyes.

Chapter Thirty

ED

I'm utterly exhausted. Meetings all day, and some prick stole my wireless charger from my desk, so my phone has died. I borrowed Alex's to charge it whilst I was in my last meeting, which took four hours!

It's after eight before I sit back down at my desk. Before checking my emails, I check my phone. I haven't been able to message Kiera this afternoon to tell her my meetings were dragging and that I would be home a little later. We normally meet after work to travel home together.

I see the message about heading for a drink. Then I see the message asking where I am, and a pang of guilt runs through me.

I see three messages from my dad, along with five missed calls and voice messages. I immediately call my dad back without listening to the messages. He takes an age to answer.

"Ed, where have you been?" My dad sounds breathless, making me instantly alert.

"Dad, what's up?"

"I had a call this afternoon from Noel's facility. He managed to persuade a young doctor to sign his release forms. His regular doctor has been away and said his progress didn't seem right to him." A grave feeling settles in the pit of my stomach as I wait for my dad to continue. I'm already packing up the rest of my stuff and transferring the call to my headphones so I can move more quickly.

"This other doctor is new, young and apparently got sucked in by his charm. She signed the release papers this morning, advising he's made such amazing progress that he can reintegrate into the outside world without assistance." I can hear his voice shake. "They found her passed out in the consultation room with severe injuries to her stomach. It looks like he got what he wanted and beat her until she passed out."

The resentment that rises is like lava rising through a volcano, ready to erupt into a violent fury of fire and destruction. "Dad, where is he?" My words sound harsh. I can't help it.

"We don't know. Police are on the lookout. He's vanished."

It's at that moment I get a call from Jess, too. She doesn't normally call me. I merge the calls without thinking twice. "Jess, what's up? You're on with me and my dad."

"I called Kiera, and when she picked up, I think I heard a man mumbling in the background. It sounded like she dropped her phone, and her phone's gone dead. Her last location was home. I feel like she's in trouble, Ed. We're getting there as quickly as we can." Her voice is trembling and full of worry. When it comes to their friendship, I have no doubt Jess will have Kiera's back to the end of the earth.

"I'm on my way home. Dad, get the police there now." I hang up and run out of the office, flagging down a cab. It'll be quicker than getting the tube. On my ten-minute ride home, my rage, anxiety, worry and every other emotion I possess when it comes to her is coming to the surface. But I can't go storming in. I need a plan. Jess texts me to say they're outside, and Dad texts to say the police are on their way.

We're around the corner at some temporary traffic lights, and I decide it will be quicker to run. I throw money at the driver, get out and sprint home. Jess is by the front door when I get there. I glance up at our apartment and notice only the bedroom light is on.

"Ed, what's happening? Why was your dad on the phone, too?" I can see the tears in her eyes. Gavin has an arm wrapped protectively around her.

"My brother got out. When we last spoke, I believed he was doing okay. But he's faked his recovery. I'm guessing he's come after Kiera. She really rattled him at the BBQ and made him lose his temper. It's not something I've known him to do in public before." I came to that conclusion whilst I was on the phone with my dad. There's no way this is a coincidence.

Jess waits outside for the police whilst Gavin and I walk up to the apartment. Gavin has his headphones in so she can hear everything and relay it to the police when they *finally* get here.

I force my body to relax a little. My shaking has settled, and my breathing has levelled out by the time I get to the front door. I open it and enter with Gavin behind me, staying out of sight.

"Kiera? You home, love?" I try to keep my voice as normal as possible to avoid suspicion.

I hear movement in the bedroom, but I can't hear Kiera. I dump my bag in the kitchen and walk into our bedroom slowly. If he's still here, I don't want him to make any sudden movements.

The sight before me would be truly erotic if it wasn't for the current situation. Kiera is lying on our bed, her hands handcuffed and tethered to the head-board. She's wearing purple lacy underwear that I haven't seen before. However, her mouth has a strip of duct tape across it, and her eyes are wild and angry. *There's my girl.*

Her gaze darts to me, widening as if silently telling me something. I hold my index finger to my lips, giving her what I hope is a reassuring smile. The hairs on the back of my neck stand up when I feel another presence in the room.

Appearing from beside the wardrobe, Noel smirks at me with the sadistic, sickening smile he used to give me before beating the shit out of me. He walks over to Kiera and looks back at me.

"You have a fiery one here, brother." His voice slides over me like slug mucus. I contain my shiver of disgust and stand silently, taking in the environment and the potential risks. Noel leans over Kiera and licks her shoulder, breathing her in at her neck, all whilst staring at me. My body is thrumming with anger, and my lips twitch up at the corners.

I'm no longer a frightened little boy, dear brother.

Chapter Thirty-One

KIERA

The relief that rushes over me when I hear Ed's voice come through the front door is palpable. My muscles are tight and sore from being manhandled and restrained by Noel and from trying to control my body so it doesn't shake. If Ed knew that Noel had undressed me, taken his time to rake his soulless dead eyes over my naked body, and then dressed me in the underwear he'd bought, Ed would lose his absolute shit.

The underwear is making me itch. The material itself is perfectly fine, but it's the lasting effect of his touch on me. The fact that Noel bought it has created this negative physical reaction in my body. Ed is walking through the apartment, but I can hear something else. I've become attuned to the sounds of our apartment, and I know Ed isn't alone. But whoever is with him doesn't come through the bedroom door. They're silent in the background somewhere.

The fury in Ed's eyes is barely contained when he sees me, but there's something else mixed in, arousal possibly. Let's face it, this is definitely one of his kinks. He and Noel are currently in a stare-off. Noel is making no sudden movements and has yet to say a word. Looking back and forth between the two, I notice Ed's mouth twitch slightly barely noticeable. Knowing that Ed is no longer afraid of Noel means this isn't going to end well...if that twitch really was a smile.

Neither of them speaks for a moment, and it feels like they're trying to see who will back down first.

"Young Kiera here was just going to demonstrate how submissive she can be." Noel makes my skin crawl. His eyes are darker than the last time I saw him, with deep shadows under them. It makes me think of those fantasy books where a demon has taken over a soul. If there is a demon in there, I can only guess it is fully in control now, making Noel snarl at Ed.

Ed's posture straightens, anger bristling off of him radiates in waves. He still hasn't said a word. Instead, he leans against the door frame. Noel touches my cheek with one clammy finger, and the sudden contact makes me jump. I can feel the bile rising in my throat as his finger grazes down the column of my neck, down over my clavicle to rest on the swell of my left breast. I dig my fingernails into the palm of my hand to stop myself from reacting.

"The funny thing about therapy..." Noel drawls, "...is when your regular psychiatrist is adamant you're a monster and hell-bent on keeping you locked up, the minute they go on holiday and send in a young, bend-able cover, it's amazing how easily suggestible they can be." I flick my eyes up to his face and see the slow smirk growing. He's trying to get Ed to react, but Ed is just staring, his face giving nothing away.

"It appears, dear brother, I'm cured and allowed to be back in the normal world." Noel grins. I can't imagine what it is like in a hospital like that, but the treatment hasn't worked.

"Clearly." That is the only word Ed has spoken since calling my name when he walked in.

"Your little bitch here..." Noel grabs my breast, inflicting pain. "...if it wasn't for her, I wouldn't have had to endure countless hours of talking, tests and faking my remarkable recovery. She needs to be punished."

Ed glares at Noel. The only slip in his otherwise stoic expression so far. Ed doesn't punish to get off on the pain; he punishes to provide pleasure.

Ed takes a step forward, and it's only then I notice movement behind him. It must have been the shadows playing with my eyes. I know someone else is out there, but is there more than one?

"Is that your excuse for beating that young doctor? Was it because she was a woman rather than the male therapist you've been dealing with? Did that make your pathetic ego feel better? Beating someone younger, smaller and physically weaker than you?" Ed takes another step towards his brother.

Noel moves his hand off of me by mere centime-tres and balls it into a fist.

"Did you charm her into signing the paperwork to release you? How long did it take for you to feel like a man again? Is this helping, Noel?" Ed sounds like he has tasted something foul. "Do you feel all manly now that you've restrained Kiera? Not properly, I might add." There's a twinkle in Ed's eyes as if he's enjoying winding up his brother.

It appears to be working because I can feel the heat emanating from Noel as his body stiffens, his chest puffs out, and there's a rumbling sound coming from him. His fist has a slight tremor, and I don't think he's far from losing control.

"I know what you're doing. I also know you're not going to do anything other than watch whilst I mark this pretty little body."

Ed raises an eyebrow. "Is that right? I'm assuming you gagged her so she couldn't tell you how disappointing you are."

That's it. Noel removes a switchblade from his back pocket. The black handle is held firmly in his hand when he flips the matching black blade up. His expression is murderous as he slowly lowers the knife to my throat.

I hold my breath, and my eyes widen, silently begging for Ed to do something. Instead, Ed stands, smirks and whistles. I feel the tip of the knife being pushed into my skin. *Fuck that hurts!* Then, a trickle of blood oozes down my neck.

Chapter Thirty-Two

ED

The moment I see Kiera's blood, I leap over the corner of the bed and grab his wrist, careful not to cause any more damage to Kiera's skin. Noel doesn't seem able to react; his body is as still as a statue, his stare like one you'd see on a deer in headlights. I rip his hand and the knife away from her without leaving an additional mark and throw the knife to the other side of the room towards the door. I've become stronger, but he's snapped out of his statue state and tries to overpower me.

The moment I bolt towards Noel and remove the knife, the police officers that Gavin let into the apartment try to tear us apart, but we're still thrashing, trying to hurt each other. There are now two officers on each of us, holding us back and pushing us to different corners of the bedroom. For a moment, I see Noel's eyes widen in what I hope is fear. It's almost like he honestly thought he could get away with this and not suffer from the consequences. Once I'm calm and the officers feel confident I'm not going to rampage towards Noel again, I'm free to move to Kiera.

Gavin has covered her in a blanket and has removed the restraints that were tying her handcuffed hands to the headboard. He doesn't have the key for the cuffs, though. When I examine her more closely, blood is dripping from her wrists. I was so focused on Noel I hadn't noticed. I internally chastise myself.

The officers are hauling Noel to his feet. "Key, now," I order.

He smirks and almost looks deranged. "In my boxers. I was going to make her get it with her tongue."

In my head, I punch him in the stomach and the balls. He doubles over, retching. But in reality, I can't afford to be detained by the police. I still smile at that thought, though, as one of the officers searches for the key and finds it in his back pocket. Bastard.

I don't miss the scowl one of the officers, who is photographing the scene, gives me, but I ignore him to release Kiera from her restraints. Picking her up in the bridal position, I carry her to the sofa so the para-medics can look her over. Gavin is grabbing her some clothes. He's a good man, from what I know anyway. This is one of the few interactions we've had with each other, though. And it's one I'll never forget.

"Kiera." He kisses the top of her head before his eyes gaze off into the distance, looking distracted.

"Yes, come up."

We look at Gavin puzzled, and then I remember

Jess has been in his ear the whole time. Within two minutes, I hear Jess shouting and watch her hurtle herself into the apartment at a speed that has me fearing she'll go through the wall. I can only assume she yelled at a police officer that she was coming up no matter what.

She grabs her friend, and they embrace. It's then that Kiera is wracked by sobs. No words are exchanged, just an embrace. Through thick and thin, they are sisters tied with something stronger than blood.

Gavin and Jess don't leave until after the police have taken all of our statements. It's well after two in the morning, and we're all exhausted. I offered to let them stay on the sofa tonight, but they wanted to give Kiera some space. Kiera is in my hoody and her loose shorts, and she is curled up against my side. I know what Noel did to her, undressing… I can't think about it; otherwise, I'll hunt him down and kill him.

She is ashamed of how easily he overpowered her. Kiera felt something was off but, in her own words, "carried on towards the danger like a dumb blonde in a shitty horror movie." I offer my silence and arms to curl up in whilst she processes. It's all I can do to settle the pure rage rattling around inside of me. I feel Kiera's weight get heavier against me, and I shuffle forward so I can lean in and pick her up. Taking her to bed and tucking her in, I call my dad to update him. Outrage is too mild for what he is feeling. I end the call after a good twenty minutes, telling him we'll catch up tomorrow. I need to be by her side. I sneak into bed next to Kiera quietly so I don't wake her, and within minutes, my fatigue takes over, and I'm pulled into a fitful sleep.

Waking up around ten, I fire off an email to both mine and Kiera's managers advising we wouldn't be in for the rest of the week, giving them a very brief overview of what happened. After, I get up to make a coffee and something to eat, realising I haven't eaten since lunchtime yesterday, leaving Kiera to sleep some more.

I set myself up at the breakfast bar, reading whilst Kiera rests. It's around noon when I hear her footsteps padding into the kitchen from the bedroom. Lifting my head, I'm surprised to see her cheery smile.

"Morning!" she chirps.

"Afternoon? How are you feeling?"

Kiera is making herself a coffee and turns to me with a serious expression on her face. "I'm alright, Ed. Nothing happened. Well, other than being undressed, changed and then restrained against my will. But nothing terrible happened, so let's move past it." Her smile is genuine, but I find myself wondering how she can get over something so quickly? It's not even been twenty-four hours.

"Okaaayyy. I mean, I understand wanting to move on, but it's still a big deal. We haven't even talked about what happened. *I'm* still processing it all." I don't mean to sound harsh, but the way her eyes widened and her brows furrowed as her shoulders drooped tells me it came out worse than I intended.

"Ed, your brother is a dick. No two ways about it.

He faked his recovery so he could hurt me because I was the one who made him lose his temper, and then people saw him for who he was. We then made a spotlight shine down on it brighter than the Blackpool Tower. He overpowered me and made me feel dirty and horrible, but then you showed up. Did you notice him shaking slightly when you wouldn't talk?"

I cock my head at her. No, I hadn't noticed that. I can't say it doesn't please me.

She smiles sweetly and continues, "The power has shifted. He's in custody now rather than a swanky psycho hospital, and he'll hopefully get what he deserves."

Death isn't in the cards for him, unfortunately.

Chapter Thirty-Three

KIERA

It takes some persuading, but I think Ed finally believes I'm okay. Honestly, I feel like I should be more upset, but I am alright. Yeah, what happened sucked, but there's nothing I can do to change it, and if I did magic up a time machine to change what happened, he'd still have come after me. He was very clear that I'd pay.

Leaving Ed to his reading, I take a nice long shower so I can change the bandages on my wrists and neck. The only wounds that piece of shit inflicted, thankfully, but they sting like a bitch in the shower. I try to enjoy the hot water running down my skin. I close my eyes and attempt to surrender to it, but my body can't relax. Ed has been very careful and hands-off since last night, but I need to feel him on me. I need the contact more than anything. I call for him, and he is there quickly.

"Were you waiting outside?" I tilt my head slightly to the side.

"I might have been passing as you called." He raises an eyebrow as he crosses his arms across his chest, smirking. *Passing my ass.*

"Well, get your arse in here. I need to feel you."

As if a tornado has swirled through our bathroom, his clothes are off and scattered across the floor, and he steps into the shower with me.

Ed pulls my back to his chest and holds me under the stream of water. His arms tighten around my waist as he buries his face in my neck, and I lay my head back on his shoulder, feeling everything around me. I feel safe, warm and secure; even the pain in my wrists has gone. My neck isn't too bad, either.

It's strange to me that in just over a year, a person can feel like home. Not our apartment or our belongings, but him. Ed grounds me in a way I've never experienced before. I can *feel* when I'm with him. Before our friendship turned into a relationship, I felt emotions, but never this deeply, and as cliché as it sounds, he makes me feel whole.

As I'm engulfed by Ed and the water and steam, Ed's hand glides up my body. I lean into him more, his erection nestling in between my butt cheeks, and I automatically rock my ass against him.

"Be careful, Missy; otherwise, I'm not going to last long. This is one place I haven't claimed yet," he says in a gravelly tone, which makes me so slick I can feel my juices on my thighs. Ed dips his fingers into my pussy, angling my ass out of the spray, and coating them in my come, humming as he pulls them out, and he gently teases my tight ring of muscles with his finger, which makes me push back a little. A growl emanates from his chest, telling me how turned on he is. I've never thought about anal before. He's teased me, but we've not gone there, and I haven't with anyone else either. A part of me is curious and wants to try, and when he leaves his finger completely still, I push myself onto it more. I'm extremely turned on as his other hand plays with my breast.

Vibrating with a newfound confidence and level of arousal, I push back further until he's breached the wall of muscle. My body aches for more as I slowly slide myself on and off his finger.

Ed suddenly slams me against the shower wall. "Kiera," he groans in my ear, sending shivers of pleasure down my spine. He takes over, circling with one finger before gently stretching me with a second. The burn is both uncomfortable and a little painful, as well as delicious. My moan reverberates off the tiles. He continues moving his fingers around gently, opening them like scissors to stretch me and help me get used to it. I'm not sure if it takes minutes or hours, but by the time he has stretched me with the third finger, my body feels everything, and it wants more. Damn, this one is stinging, and my God, I feel full, stretched, and I can't tell which way is up with the pain and pleasure he's causing.

Placing my hands above me on the wall, Ed tells me to keep them there or else. I'm on high alert, my pain and pleasure sensors are short-circuiting, and I want him in me. I'm told to be patient as he steps out of the shower. When he returns seconds later, I feel something cold flowing between my ass cheeks, which is nice compared to the slight burning. I flinch at the sensation, and he kisses my neck and gently pushes his fingers back in. "Don't worry, I just needed to get some lube to help."

When I'm moaning and pushing back on Ed's hand, he adds another finger, and I notice how gentle he's being. Ed teases, stretches and squirts more lube onto his fingers, sliding them in and out of me, waiting until I'm pushing back for more before he removes his fingers and replaces them with the tip of his cock. It is a little painful. Taking his time, he pushes a little more.

"Jesus, Kiera." His voice is raspy.

Each nudge causes a burning sensation that makes me wince. Ed's fingers find my clit and rub it, relaxing my muscles and giving me pleasure before he begins to move again. I never thought I'd enjoy anal, but, my God, I feel so full and stretched as he slowly rocks his hips and circles my clit at the same time. His free hand grasps my hip tight enough to bruise me. I can tell he's trying to control himself so I won't get hurt, but at the same time, I want more.

"Easy love, I'm not even halfway in yet."

"What??" I can't believe that. I don't think I can take all of him.

He continues, slow and gentle, playing with my clit at the same time. I can feel the pressure building up in my core. One, two, three more strokes on my clit, and I come undone. My orgasm is powerful, and there are white spots in my vision.

"FUCK!" Ed shouts as I feel him pulsing in me. He slows to a stop, and other than the shower, all I can hear is our laboured breathing. Damn, that was intense.

Ed leans his forehead on my shoulder, his breathing slowly returning to normal. We clean ourselves up and turn off the shower.

"That was the hottest thing I've ever done in the shower. We'll work you up to take all of me." He grins as he pulls me into him and kisses me.

I never want to not see this man undone. I love him when he's raw, and it's then I feel like things are too good to be true. We're happy, in a really good place, and I don't want anything to mess that up.

The next couple of months are just like this, happy...until we get the phone call that changes Ed from my controlled, beautiful boyfriend into a raging mess.

Chapter Thirty-Four

KIERA

The thunderclouds are rolling in over Ed, and the storm that's brewing inside him feels dangerous. We both received phone calls this morning. Ed had a call from his dad giving him a heads-up that the court case was going to start soon. Noel had been found fit for trial, although we've been warned the defence team is good and will try to claim he was mentally incapacitated. We both received a call from the prosecution team, and we're both to bear witness against his brother. His ability to lie and manipulate his way through life so far has me feeling unnerved about it all.

Ed's mood has gone from bad to worse with each meeting we have had with the prosecution team. They rile him up like the defence team would, saying a child could make up all sorts of stories, and, of course, his girlfriend would lie to protect him. The defence team will try to impeach his credibility as a witness. Although his parents have given statements, they

174

cannot claim testament to the acts they were blind to for years. And whilst Noel is standing trial for his abuse against Steph, other women who have come forward, and myself, not to mention the breaking and entering and holding me hostage, Ed has experience with Noel from when they were children, making him an excellent character witness. It can prove Noel has been abusive and psychotic for years. This information may not be enough to bring Noel down, but the prosecution team is adamant it will paint a picture for the judge and jury. Noel's character stems from early years, and that trying to blame his actions on his mental health is bullshit.

The trial doesn't start until the new year, but I feel like it could take a few weeks to go through evidence and witnesses once we are in court.

Over the next week, Ed is quiet. He's barely looked at me, let alone touched me. I can't imagine what he's going through mentally, but I'm in this with him, not against him.

It's a dreary Saturday morning when he's on his laptop in the office. I lean against the door frame, watching him, worrying about him.

"What?" His tone is clipped, and with the deep frown wrinkling his brow and downturn to his mouth, he looks pissed.

"Just making sure you're okay." My voice is soft, but I can't help the hurt that comes through.

"I'm fine. Stop hovering." That cut like a thousand tiny papercuts over my skin.

"I know you're stressed and going through a lot,

Ed, but you do NOT get to take it out on me." Without waiting for his reply, I grab my bag and go out. I'm not staying in this negative energy field he's created.

I get halfway down our street before I look behind me. He hasn't tried to come after me. A tear escapes as I carry on walking. I continue until my feet ache, and by the time I look up to take in my surroundings, I've made it into central London. I've been wandering around without noticing the time. I grab a coffee and sit outside the café to watch the world go by. I check my phone, and there aren't any messages or calls from Ed. Jess is out tonight with Gavin, and I'm sure Sarah and Jake are busy. It makes me a little sad knowing I don't have a huge circle of friends, but I've always believed in keeping my circle small and real.

Why does time fly when you're buried in your head? By the time I finish my second coffee and a croissant, three hours have passed since I left. Still no word from Ed. I decide to call my mum. She is always a ray of sunshine when I feel like I am in the middle of an oceanic storm.

"Hey, sweetie. How are you?"

"I'm alright, Mum. Just wanted to hear your voice." The wobble in my voice is evident. I need a cuddle.

"Come over, sweetheart. I'm just cooking a shepherd's pie."

"I love you, mum."

I pay my bill and take the train over to Mum and Dad's. The smell of home hits me when I walk through the front door. I haven't lived here in years, but the aroma of my mum's cooking, along with whatever scent is in the house, is like a blanket of comfort wrapping around me.

I stroll into the kitchen to find my mum removing her mouth-watering shepherd's pie from the oven. The top is brown and crispy. Perfect. I can practically feel the drool escaping my mouth as I head towards her and kiss her on the cheek.

Mum doesn't ask why I'm here. Instead, she grabs me a can of Coke from the fridge and serves me a portion of food. My dad meanders into the kitchen as if following his nose. The smile on his face grows when he sees me sitting at the table.

"Kiera, I didn't know you were coming today." His arms encircle me from behind, and he plants a kiss on the top of my head.

"Well, when I called, Mum said what she was cooking, and I headed straight over."

"That man of yours not feeding you enough? He'll learn." My dad chuckles, knowing full well what the term "hangry" meant before it got popular. I still feel a pang of pain at the mention of Ed. Still no word from him.

The three of us sit at the table and wolf down our food. Mum really does have a talent for making me feel better, not just with her presence but with her food. After a couple of hours of hanging out with my parents, I bid my goodbyes and head to the door. My dad's tidying up the kitchen whilst my mum wraps her hand around my wrist.

"Is everything okay? You sounded upset earlier."

"I'm okay, Mum. Ed's just had a bad week, and his mood was annoying me." I force a smile to try to convince her and give her another hug before walking out the door and to the station. I'm sitting on the train on my way home, wondering what mood will await me when I arrive.

Chapter Thirty-Five

ED

Kiera returned home an hour ago and went straight into the bathroom for a shower. I have no idea what she's doing in there, but nothing should take an hour. When I knock on the door to ask if she's okay, all I get is a "Yep" in response. Infuriating!

I head back to the office, pouring myself into reports to calm the throbbing vein in my head. I love her more than life itself, but storming out and coming back late is just childish. Yes, I was short with her, but she normally sticks around our apartment.

When I finally hear her come out of the bathroom, I give her some space to get dressed. My frustration is growing. It's not her fault. I've been sent emails from my solicitor with Noel's statement, preparing me for court. It's made the anger within me visceral, and I can't shake it. It is to the point that everything is forcing it closer to the surface. Even the tapping sound coming from my keyboard makes me want to smash the thing to smithereens.

That's why I haven't touched Kiera in what feels like years. I don't trust myself not to take it out on her in the bedroom. My only release, which will instantly make me feel calmer, and I deny myself. Something else to add to the things that are pissing me off.

Kiera comes out of our bedroom dressed in a crop top and shorts. My hands twitch to touch her. The heat coming from her eyes could be weaponised. It isn't sexual heat; it's anger, which makes me twitch more. I love it when she's feisty. I walk over to her carefully, my movements methodical like a panther.

"What's up?" I try to make my voice soft, but it comes out brittle.

"Really? What's up? No 'I'm sorry for snapping and taking this shitty situation out on you?' No 'I'm sorry for not touching you in over a week?' No 'Where did you go this afternoon?'" Her arms are crossed in front of her chest, bringing those beautiful tits bouncing up higher.

I want to touch her. I want to tell her I'm sorry for being an ass this week. I want to tell her that, even when she's mad, she brightens my day like nothing else in this universe.

But I don't. I stare at her, my vein threatening to jump from my head to strangle the defiance right out of her. My voice comes out colder than Antarctica. "You went to your parents like a damn child. You wanted to feel something other than mad at me. What? You wanted me to chase after you?"

The look on her face pierces my heart with a thousand needles coated in TCP, that fowl-smelling antiseptic liquid we grew up with in the 90s. A whirl of emotions flashes through her eyes in the span of seconds. The most prominent ones are the worst. Shock. Sadness. Anger.

"Fuck you, Ed." All I feel is the whoosh of air as she storms past me, and our bedroom door slams shut, rattling the walls.

"You prick," I chastise myself before settling on the sofa for the night. There's no way she's going to entertain sharing a bed with me after that shit show.

IT'S BEEN TWELVE DAYS, EIGHT HOURS AND AROUND twenty minutes since I last touched Kiera. The frostiness of our apartment is rivalling the turn of winter outside. I miss her, her smile, her touch and her laugh. She hasn't left. We're just co-existing together. How on earth did I fuck this up? Oh yeah. My spawn of Satan brother. Just thinking about him brings my heart rate up to an alarming level. It used to be from fear, but now, it's from unbridled rage. I can't blame all my actions on him. Did he have an influence on who I am today? Yes. Did I not spend years trying to make myself a better person? Also yes.

Yes, he's caused me to feel all sorts of anger, but I'm the dick that directed that at Kiera. Not him. I need to do better if I want to keep her.

Christmas is four weeks away, and court is in six.

The date is imprinted on my mind, ensuring I get next to no sleep. I've been riddled with nightmares, and regardless of her anger, Kiera always rolls over to comfort me. I went back to sleeping in bed with her two nights after our argument.

Five in the morning, and I'm wide awake and drenched in sweat. My beautiful tractor is sleeping next to me as I rise to take a shower. I trace my eyes over her sleeping form. She truly is beautiful, even when she sounds like she is demolishing a building. After allowing myself a couple of minutes of peace watching Kiera sleep, I head to the shower.

As I stand under the hot stream of water, my mind races. What if he gets away with the hurt he's caused? I'm not concerned about my past—the dick isn't on trial for that—but what about the others he's hurt? What if he comes after Kiera again? He blames her for his inevitable arrest, but it was his sloppiness that got him caught. I stand there for a few more minutes, running scenarios through my head before I quickly wash and step out. And then I feel like I'm being watched.

When I find her, the anger suddenly dissipates. I wrap the towel around my waist and saunter out to her. Her wary eyes watch me.

"You need to take a break from torturing yourself." Her voice is soft, her body rigid.

I give in and wrap my arms around her waist, resting my head on her shoulder. It takes a few beats, but her body softens as her arms wrap around me. We stand like that for a while before my back starts to ache. I straighten and cup her cheek.

"I'm sorry, love. You deserve so much more than this. More than me."

Tears well in her eyes as she leans into my touch. "We're a team, dumbass. Start treating us like one." After placing a kiss on my palm, she moves out of my grasp and into the kitchen, where I can hear her start up the coffee machine.

I go into our bedroom, feeling...empty suddenly. The anger and fear that has consumed me for weeks has dissolved into a small ball in the pit of my stomach. I didn't realise how much I was holding on to, especially with Kiera. I manage to put on my boxers before crashing back into bed and giving in to exhaustion.

Chapter Thirty-Six

KIERA

When I check in on Ed, I find him crashed out on our bed, so I let him sleep whilst I potter about. It's nearly midday, and I'm getting a little restless. I decide to walk down to our local café and get us some lunch. Leaving him a quick note, I grab my keys and go.

The air has turned cold, but it's not raining, thankfully. It always amazes me how our little island gets so much rain. As I walk down our road, the brisk wind whipping my hair around my face, I hope Ed can start to process what's going on. In the space of a year, he's had a lot to process. Our relationship, the whole shit show with his brother from the BBQ to the arrest, not to mention the escape and re-arrest, then court, and finally facing the feelings Ed's buried for years. That's a lot for anyone to go through.

I bustle into the café, feeling pushed in by the wind. I overhear two older gentlemen talking about the storm that's coming tonight, and I can't help but think about the storm that's coming in the new year. I order our food and flick through my social media as I wait. I read the email earlier in the week from the solicitors regarding the court date, but it's something I shoved into a box until after Christmas. This is our first one together, and I'd love to take Ed's mind off of the case.

By the time I make it home, I resemble an extra from *Oliver*. My hair looks like a bird's nest, my scarf has unravelled, and I'm thankful I chose not to wear makeup today as I fear it would be smeared across my face. I poke my nose into our room to see Ed still sleeping. I drape a blanket over him and quietly leave the room.

I grab my sandwich and latte, curl up on the sofa and flick through Netflix, nostalgia hitting me. I can remember when I used to order DVDs from them and post them back. Now, I have their entire library at my fingertips. A small smile warms my cold face. It's the little things that make me happy.

By three in the afternoon, Ed still isn't awake, but I'm feeling sleepy, so I decide to crawl into bed next to him and have a siesta. Since he's crashed on the bed diagonally, I spoon him, wrapping my arm and leg over him like a koala. His body feels rigid at first, but then I feel his muscles relax the longer I hold him. It doesn't take me long to drift off.

THREE WEEKS UNTIL CHRISTMAS AND I HAVEN'T bought a single present. I'm normally the organised one who has shopped and has everything wrapped by the end of October. I'm scrolling shamelessly through Amazon for some nice presents. I'm not going big this year: Mum, Dad, Ed and his parents. I've picked out some nice perfume and bath bombs for Mum, Dad gets his annual slippers and Scotch, Ed's parents are getting a nice hamper with teas, coffees and biscuits, and I'm completely stuck on Ed. What do you get for the person who has everything?

As I'm scrolling, Ed comes into the living room and slumps on the sofa next to me. He's still not himself, but at least his aura isn't an angry demon trying to suck my soul from me.

"Do you have a Christmas list?" I eye him over my phone. He looks bored with the conversation already, but I'm going to buy his gift today. Whether it's something he wants or just a random gift is up to him.

"No, I haven't made one since I was a kid. What's on your list?"

I laugh. He knows me well. I did indeed write lists for my birthday and Christmas. I do like to be organised. "I shared the note with you the other week. Is there anything you'd like for Christmas?"

Ed's eyes scour over me. His thoughts are unreadable, as are his emotions, but it doesn't stop goosebumps from prickling my skin. "You," he says, not tearing his gaze away from mine.

"You have me, don't be daft. Give me an inkling?"

He leans over and kisses me, his lips soft at first,

then he adjusts his position and sinks deeper into the kiss. We've kissed since our little argument, but not properly, and he still hasn't touched me. If I was more self-conscious, my mind would trigger all sorts of scenarios. But I know he always needs to be in control, and with how frustrated he's been, he hasn't been in control of his emotions.

Ed picks my phone out of my hand and tosses it on the table without breaking our mouths apart. He pushes his weight onto me more so that I'm lying with my back on the sofa, his kiss becoming more urgent. His lips bruise mine as his tongue licks my bottom lip, silently asking for entry. I grant the access he wants and needs. A desperate sob escapes me as he bites my bottom lip. I've missed this so much. I push my breasts up into his chest and wrap my legs around his waist, needing to feel his full weight on me.

Ed grasps the nape of my neck and angles my head backwards roughly. His teeth graze my ear and along my neck to that sweet little spot where he bites down. "Oww!" I'm panting through the pain, which turns to pleasure as he sucks on the wound he's inflicted. My hips instinctively twitch against him. I can feel his arousal vibrating through his body, especially the rock-hard erection between us.

When Ed finally releases my mouth, I breathe in some much-needed air. "I've missed you," I mutter breathlessly. It sounds like I've been running a marathon and not kissing my boyfriend on our sofa.

"I've missed you, too," Ed says before capturing my mouth again. Our kiss soon becomes frantic, and my hands are roaming his back before settling in his hair, messing it up.

Ed growls into my mouth when I raise my hips, grinding myself against his erection, needing the friction. It's been too long since we've been intimate. I feel feral with need.

Chapter Thirty-Seven

ED

It's been weeks since I've allowed myself to touch Kiera. My balls are practically blue, and I'm going to blow my load before we even start if she keeps rubbing herself against me. My girl needs to be taken care of thoroughly before I get any attention, though. I've been selfish and need to bury myself in her. I break our kiss, and my lips are swollen, but I don't give a fuck as I kiss, lick and nip my way down her jaw, pulling her t-shirt up as I move towards her breasts. I've missed her glorious tits. I paw at them with the gentleness of an escaped prisoner. My rough touch elicits a gasp from her, making her back arch and pushing them further into my hands.

I bow my head and lick the dip in her cleavage. The salty taste of sweat is already lining her skin. Utterly delicious. I take my time and lick my way across both of her breasts. Those rosy nipples turn into hardened points. I kiss my way down her ribs, across her stomach and smile against her skin as her breaths become shallow.

Leaning back on my heels, I make quick work of her jeans, tearing them off her body and tossing them to the floor. I don't have the patience to take her underwear off. Staring into her eyes, the desire firing behind them flares into an inferno as I rip her underwear and discard them somewhere over the back of the sofa.

"Oi, they were comfy!" Kiera complains, but the tone in her voice is playful, and her body is practically vibrating with need. I can smell her already.

I kiss my way from her belly button down to her thighs and feel her shiver under my touch. I roughly part her legs further, my hands holding her thighs down as I run my nose over her, inhaling her scent. "Fucking perfect." I lose any remaining restraint as I dive into her folds with my tongue. Her body jerks and I firmly keep her still. Licking her up and down, Kiera's moans break the silence we've had around us for weeks.

I take my time, circling her clit with the tip of my tongue. I apply just the right amount of pressure as I slowly tease her entrance with my finger. I can feel how wet she is for me already. "Good girl." I raise my head slightly to see her hooded gaze. Dipping back down, I feast on her like she's my last meal. Sliding my finger into her, she releases a loud moan as she pushes herself further onto my hand. I slowly slide one finger out and push two into her whilst my tongue twirls around her clit, lapping up her juices. I'd happily die right now.

I work Kiera into a frenzy, edging her over and over again until she is panting. "Ed, please," she breathlessly begs. I'm not punishing her by edging her orgasm; I want her to see stars. I bring her to the edge one more time before slowing down. Kiera whimpers, and a tear slips from her eye.

I push my fingers into her again, curling them to hit that spot she needs for release. "Come for me, baby," I order and suck her clit into my mouth whilst pushing on that spot. She explodes around me, screaming my name so loud I'll be surprised if the neighbours don't complain. The force of her orgasm squeezes me like a vice, making my fingers feel as if they are about to break, but I continue to pump them in and out, forcing her to ride out her orgasm as she trembles.

I don't allow her much time to recover before I discard my jeans and hike her legs over my shoulders. I plunge deep and feel like I'm about to come from the heat surrounding me. I still for a moment, visualising Excel formulas in my head so this doesn't end too quickly. As soon as I am safe to carry on, I thrust.

As much as I want this to last longer, I can feel my climax building. But I can't come until I feel her come around my cock. I lean back on my heels and run the pad of my thumb over her clit. She clenches around me. "Come for me, baby. I'm not gonna last much longer."

Kiera's orgasm ricochets through her, and I come with her, groaning her name, making my throat sore. I collapse on top of her, my dick still inside her, until our breathing returns to normal. Even then, we lay there, the sofa covered in our combined juices.

Kiera strokes my hair with one hand, and her other traces invisible patterns on my back. I lift my head to kiss her gently this time. I pull out of her, and she sits up with me. Our stomachs rumble in unison, eliciting a laugh from both of us, and I notice it's past eight in the evening. No wonder we're hungry.

"I'm already ordering takeout. Mexican okay?" Kiera's thumbs work fast on her phone. I've learnt very quickly that nothing gets between my girl and her food.

"I love you." I plant a kiss on her whilst she stares at her phone before I wander into the kitchen to fix us a drink.

After dinner, we lie in bed, sated and full. I feel much lighter than I have in weeks. I needed her connection and stupidly denied myself. With Kiera's head on my chest, I enjoy the closeness we've been missing. I am about to tell her as much when those engine noises escape from her. Chuckling to myself, I lean over to turn off the light and discover that sleep comes easily for me tonight. All I need is her and to get out of my head.

Chapter Thirty-Eight

KIERA

Two weeks until Christmas, and I still don't have any idea of what to get Ed. Our plans are set, but I'm stumped for a gift. For Christmas, we are going to wake up together, then go to our parents' houses separately, and we will get back together in the evening. On Boxing Day, we're going to his parents' for lunch and mine for dinner. Yes, I organise my holidays around food.

I'm in the city today. With Christmas coming up, a lot of our major campaigns are done at work, which means a slower workday. It gives me time to run to Starbucks on my lunch break. As I'm wandering down the street in my own little world, I stumble across an antique shop I haven't seen before. My steps falter as I spy a watch, and my feet take me into the store as I picture the watch on Ed's wrist. He does like his watches.

I speak to the man who owns the shop, John, who

I'm guessing is in his late seventies. I'm looking at the silver watch with a brass inner skeleton showing through the face. I've seen watches like this before, but the bit that caught my eye was the engraved letters on the bracelet. *K & E.* It's like I was meant to find this for Ed.

As John talks to me about the watch, I pretend to understand what he's saying. "…antique piece… only one hundred of these made…classic time-piece…" I blush, imagining the watch glinting from Ed's wrist as he wraps his hand round my neck as I come. I shake my head and try to listen to John. He's a sweet man. Now, he's telling me about his family and showing me a picture of them on the wall behind his desk.

I'm starting to get nervous about giving this as a present to Ed. "Be honest with me, John. Do you think a man who has everything will love this as a Christmas present?"

"With a woman like you, Kiera, the man has the world. You could give him a bar of used soap, and he'd be happy." John gives me a sweet smile, and strangely, I believe him.

"Okay, I'll take it." I push my credit card over to him as he boxes up the watch.

I get distracted by the other items in John's shop whilst he's wrapping Ed's present. Why I never noticed this place before, I don't know, but I'm glad I did today. When I turn around, John's eyes are sparkling with mischief; he looks like he is bouncing and has a grin on his face.

"Why do I feel like you're up to something?" I smile at him.

"This is the last week my store will be open. I threw in a little something special for you to wear to match your man's new accessory."

I tear up a little at both John's admission about his shop closing just as I've discovered it and that he has been kind enough to gift me something as well. I smile again, trying to hold back my emotions and thank him before leaving.

I don't peek until I'm home. When I do, I tear up again. John didn't gift me a "little something." He boxed up a gorgeous silver necklace with a cage pendant that encases a gorgeous blue opal. I immediately put it on and admire my new piece of jewellery in the mirror, emotions clogging my throat.

———

It's Christmas Eve, and all of the presents are wrapped and in the bag I'll have to drag to Mum and Dad's tomorrow. I've hired a car for a couple of days as trains will be non-existent over the holidays. Ed has wrapped his presents, and they're already in his car. I still have cello tape stuck to my boob from the end of the roll I fought with earlier.

Ed and I sit on the sofa, scrolling through the true crime section on Netflix, typical Christmas viewing and all that. His anger seems to be more under control, but I can feel the storm brewing. New Year, new me? No chance. New Year…Noel's trial starts, and I know shit is going to hit the fan and completely test our relationship. I hope we are strong enough to pull through it. Ed feels on edge, though. Something is bristling under that cool mask he has on his face. He appears to be concentrating on scrolling through his phone, but his eyes are restless, flicking between the TV and me.

After watching a seemingly dull murder documentary, I stretch my arms over my head like a cat, my bones cracking in delight, and I signal that I'm ready for bed. I pad barefoot into the bathroom and brush my teeth, ready to curl under the blanket before the mayhem starts tomorrow morning. When I reach the bedroom, I stumble to a stop in the doorway. Our entire bed is covered in petals, colours ranging from orange, red, pink, purple and red. In the middle is a little box. My heart falters. We weren't doing presents until tomorrow evening, and I know I go against all romcoms when I think, *I really hope that isn't a ring box.*

Ed looks nervous, and I can feel my stomach churning—the Chinese we ate for dinner is threatening to make a reappearance. I flick my gaze between Ed and the bed. There's a small smile on my face, and energy is rolling off of him, making me feel nervous. I step towards him, placing my hand on his bicep. "You okay?" He nods in response.

"Kiera…" It sounds like his throat is dry, regardless of the half-empty glass of water on his bedside table.

Oh shit.

Ed grabs the box of the bed. Even though my nerve endings feel like they're on high alert, all I'm thinking is those petals are going to be a bitch to clean up. I can already see them under the bed.

Standing straight again, Ed faces me. His eyes are glossy but focused on me. Opening the box, I spy a gorgeous white gold band with rose gold leaves wound round it. It's beautiful. I look back at Ed, my eyes wide with trepidation.

"Kiera, this isn't THE ring, but it's a promise ring. A ring to symbolise my promise to be better, especially controlling my emotions and my promise to be yours. As much as I'd love you to have my name because you are mine, neither of us is in the right place for that ring yet."

He takes the ring out of the box and places it on my left ring finger. I stare at it with tears in my eyes. I know it's not an engagement ring. He's right. We're nowhere near that stage yet. But it's a promise. That means the absolute world. I haven't said a word. Instead, I quickly close the space between us, my arms flying around his neck, and kiss him with every ounce of love I have for him.

"I love it, Ed. Thank you." I rush to the living room, reach under the small tree in the corner and grab his present. When I return to the bedroom, he looks bemused. His shoulders relax a little when he notices my present.

"My turn," I say with a mischievous grin and hand him his gift. This is the present I've been the most nervous about. I wanted to get him something perfect, and I think I did.

Chapter Thirty-Nine

ED

Kiera hands me a present, and though I don't fully understand why, I feel emotional. We exchanged birthday presents earlier this year, but it didn't feel as intimate as this. Then again, we are surrounded by petals that took me for-fucking-ever to pick off flowers. My fingertips still sting from the thorns on the rose stems.

She looks at me expectantly, and I finally tear myself out of my head long enough to open the present. She rolls her eyes. She'll get a spanking for that later. I take off the wrapping paper to reveal a burgundy leather box. It feels heavy. I carefully open the box, and my breath leaves me. I'm staring at a striking watch. The intricate details remind me of Kiera's most beautiful features. It sparkles like her eyes, and the curves on the tip of the hands remind me of her hips.

My eyes sting with tears that haven't been shed in a

long time when I notice the initials inscribed on the strap. I take it out gently and replace my current watch with this one. The weight of it is heavy enough to know you're wearing it, but not heavy enough that it will be a strain. My gaze rakes from the watch on my wrist to Kiera's fidgeting hands and then to her eyes.

I grab the nape of her neck and drag her down to the bed with me. I sit with Kiera on my lap and rest my hands on either side of her face. "It's the most beautiful present anyone has ever bought me." I mean every word. I've received watches before, lovely gifts from family, but I can *feel* the thought and love that went into finding this present.

The grin that emanates from her has enough power to light up the world, one of her many amazing qualities. I bring my mouth to hers and kiss her softly, every ounce of my love pouring into her from me. Kiera gently rocks on me. It could be a simple reflex, but I can feel her body practically vibrating. She is nothing if not passionate, and who am I to resist my woman?

With a growl that pulsates through my chest, I twist us so Kiera is lying beneath me. With one hand on the nape and the other on her hip, our kiss continues unbroken. She raises her hips to meet mine, and without a doubt in my mind, I know she can feel how hard I am for her.

I normally like to take my time with her, but tonight, I can't restrain myself. When I pry my lips from Kiera's, she's panting. I'm already leaning back and taking off her leggings, nearly ripping them in my desperation to be inside of her. My jeans come off next, along with my top. Kiera straightens up and rips her top off, followed by her bra, and throws them somewhere into the abyss of our bedroom floor.

I'm back on her within seconds, devouring her flesh with my lips and teeth. I can smell her arousal, and I slide my fingers between her slit. She is slick, and I haven't entered her yet. Without warning, I plunge two fingers inside her; at the same time, I take one of her nipples between my teeth, forcing her back to arch off the bed, and a delectable moan soars out of her mouth. She's close already.

It takes me a couple of minutes to make her scream my name. I'm not letting her come down from her orgasm before I thrust all the way inside her, making her scream again. Her nails scratch down my back as her legs wrap round my waist. I lean back on my heels and hook her knees over my elbows as I plough into her relentlessly. Her pussy is clenching around my cock, threatening to milk me dry before we're finished. I angle back slightly, knowing I've hit *that* spot when her eyes roll in the back of her head, her mouth becomes slack, and her hands grab the sheets along with the petals I haven't removed yet.

I bring my thumb down over her clit, circling, finding the right pressure that makes her moan for God, and I'm not far from coming. The emotional build-up inside me needs a release, and I'll be damned if I come before her. I work harder, hitting both spots with precision as I notice her body trembling. The tingling sensation has started at the base of my spine.

Kiera's cries and pants become shorter as she suddenly bows her back, her eyes roll, and she screams before coming so bloody hard I think she's going to cut off circulation to my cock. The masochist organ absolutely loves it, and I come hard enough to see stars.

I collapse on top of Kiera, both of us breathing hard before we finally come back to this realm of reality.

"Fuck," she says, laughing slightly breathlessly.

I capture her mouth with mine. "I fucking love you."

"I love you, too." She is still breathless, and my chest swells with pride from fucking her to the point she still can't talk properly.

I find the energy to roll off her. Both of us are covered in sweat, and the petals are sticking everywhere. We laugh before getting out of bed. Kiera goes to jump in the shower to rinse off as I clear the bed. I'm lazy and hoover the petals up. Next time, I'll save them for her. Tonight, I want to rinse off the floral decorations and sleep.

We get back into bed, and I pick a petal from Kiera's hair since she didn't bother washing it. "Sleep now, angel; otherwise, Santa won't bring you any presents." I wink at her, and she giggles.

I turn off the light and bring her into my arms. There's no better feeling than having her curled up against me, both of us sated. I close my eyes and drift off to sleep, smiling at the thought of our future children waking us up on Christmas morning with shouts of excitement, "Santa's been here!"

Chapter Forty

KIERA

On the drive to my parents, I have Michael Bublé on full blast, preparing me for the Christmas onslaught. I love Christmas and being around family, but I'm not going to lie and say I didn't bring my tracksuit bottoms to slip into later. What is it with Mum cooking enough for a small army?

I pull up to my parents' house and automatically feel relaxed. I know my digestive system is going to get a battering today, but I honestly can't wait. My mum's cooking is awesome at the best of times, but her Christmas dinner? There are always three meats, all of the trimmings, including red cabbage, bread sauce and pigs in a blanket. There are still four hours to wait for it, but my mouth is already watering.

Walking into the house, I dump the bag of gifts under the tree and head into the kitchen.

"Merry Christmas," I sing to my parents. My mum

has Alexa blaring Christmas tunes as she preps the meat, and my dad is dutifully peeling potatoes.

"Happy Christmas, darling," my mum chirps. "Coffee is in the pot."

My dad smiles at me as I kiss him on the cheek and head over to the pot of happiness to pour myself a bucketload of Italian blend. God love the Italians.

I sit in the kitchen catching up with my parents whilst they prep lunch. I know better than to get involved with my mum's dinner plan. She has everything on a timeline, and we don't mess with that.

The conversation quickly turns to Ed and me. "So, does he have good intentions?" I roll my eyes at my dad's comment. I love that he's old-fashioned in some ways, but like a lot of the older generation, he doesn't understand today's dating standards. Most men I've gone on dates with prior to Ed were vile.

"He does, Dad. He's a good guy." I absentmindedly play with the promise ring on my finger, and the motion catches my mum's attention.

"And what is that?" Her eyes dart between my ring and my dad.

"It's a promise ring, not an engagement ring. A promise that he'll always be there and try to be the best version of himself for me." I smile to myself, remembering the initial reaction to the near heart attack I had when I saw the ring box.

"That's so sweet. No one promises anything nowadays," Mum muses whilst she puts the meat in the oven.

We talk about how things have been since Ed and I

started living together and how secure we both feel. I leave out the trial and the tension it has caused at times. They don't need to worry about those details. I change the subject to gifts as dinner is now prepped, and we have some time to sit in the living room.

My parents open their gifts from Ed and me. They give me their gifts of notebooks, a new laptop bag and some makeup I can never justify buying for myself. We sit watching reruns of *Only Fools* and *Horses* whilst waiting for the food. I can smell the meat cooking, and my stomach is growling.

I reach for my phone to text Ed. I do miss him when we're not together. Maybe next year, we can have both families together for Christmas.

> Me: My stomach is protesting. I'm starving.

> Ed: Haha. Have a snack then.

> Me: And ruin dinner? You philistine!

> Ed: Oh I miss you. Are you in danger of becoming hangry?

> Me: Yes, dinner is still an hour away.

> Ed: GET A SNACK! Lives will be spared today.

> Me: Fine. I have a biscuit. I miss you x

> Ed: I miss you too. Not sure I can stay at the parents' tonight. It's very sombre here today with the upcoming shit show in a couple of weeks.

> Me: I get that. You're welcome here if you want company, otherwise I will see you tomorrow x

I tuck my phone away as Mum heads into the kitchen, and I scamper after her in the hopes I'll get to have some chef's perks, ulterior motives and all that. Mum quickly takes pity on me and throws me some snacks whilst she gets the plates ready, and then it's FINALLY time to eat.

ACCORDING TO THE STICKY TOFFEE PUDDING BOX, I now identify as a family of four because I ate the entire thing after two portions of dinner. I regret nothing. I can't move, and I may not be able to fit out of the door, but I'm sitting in my joggers, rubbing my satisfied belly whilst watching *Love Actually*. Dad's asleep in his chair, and Mum is pretending to not be sleepy as her head nods again. I'm happily stretched on the sofa, looking about six months pregnant.

I'm scrolling through the pre-Boxing Day sales, wondering what to waste my money on when a text pops up. Ed has sent me a picture of a plant. What? Before I can text back, he sends me a picture of a door. I smile and drag my ass off the sofa to waddle to the front door. As I open it, I find him standing there in dark jeans and a black shirt. I really wish I wasn't so bloated right now because he's looking hot enough to jump right here, right now.

"Hey, gorgeous." He grins, dragging me to him.

"Hey, yourself. You must have left your parents' a lot earlier than planned."

"Yeah, I missed you and wanted to see what you looked like after eating the house."

I laughed and smacked his arm hard.

Ed pulls me to him and kisses me gently. "You look as gorgeous as ever." Fucking charmer.

I drag him inside. Mum is now fully asleep in her chair, so we decide to hang out in the kitchen and leave the sleeping parents to it. Ed and I sit with a cuppa and talk about our days. He pulls me onto his lap as we peer out of the kitchen window. The sun is setting over the garden, creating a beautiful picture with hues of orange, purple and pink. At this moment, I feel nothing but happiness. Well, other than the massive need to fart now that my food is digesting. But that can wait until I take a walk outside. I don't want him to be blown away by the nuclear force that is building inside me.

Chapter Forty-One

Christmas went by in a blur, from the quiet day at my parents' to meeting Kiera at her parents' house. That in itself was a monumental moment. Not only did I get to spend some time with them, but I also discovered what an absolute powerhouse Kiera's arse is. Seriously, that woman can out-fart a lot of grown men. And the smell? That can be weaponised.

It's now New Year's Eve. We're having a quiet night in since Noel's trial starts in a week. We both want clear heads for that. We're watching some random film on Netflix, and I can feel Kiera tensing beside me, which normally means she's trying not to cry. I refocus on the TV and see Rob Lowe watching that girl from Sex and The City walk away.

I can't tell you what's going on because my mind is preoccupied with trying to organise my thoughts. Does Noel feel guilty for what he's done? Will he ever change? What if he gets away with it? Why do I feel no remorse for testifying against him, yet when I think about him spending years in prison, I feel sad? My brain is scrambled, and I need to keep a check on it, or else I'll end up pushing away the people I love.

Whilst I'm in my head, the film is scrolling through the credits, and I can feel Kiera looking at me.

"All okay up there?" she asks, running her fingers through my hair.

I lean into her touch, realising how numb I felt during the film. "I'm alright, love. My brain is running through different scenarios when all I want to do is shut them down for a bit."

Kiera straddles my lap and wraps her warm arms around me, pressing her chest into mine and nuzzling her head into my shoulder. The more I concentrate on feeling Kiera, the less numb I become. It's like all of my senses are coming back to life, and my eyes feel like they're opening slowly, similar to a new flower bud in spring. My brain is becoming more focused, and I can feel my body again.

Breathing her in, I tug her even closer to me. She is all I need. My darkness recedes when she is near. My shining light.

IT'S A GREY, DRIZZLY WEDNESDAY MORNING, AND WE'RE standing outside the courthouse in the city, unable to see much of the skyline as the mist descends upon the skyscrapers. We walk up the steps and into the building. Once we're through security, Kiera and I are shown to different rooms as we're both witnesses.

I sit on my own, waiting for the legal team to come in. I can feel the numbness falling over me, suffocating me like a weighted blanket. All of my positive feelings have been swallowed by doubt, sadness and anger. Restless, I pace the room, my feet wearing the plain brown carpet thin. By the time the paralegal comes in to see me, my face is blank, my restless energy is at bay, and my numbness has taken over.

"Good morning, Mr Green. I'm Candace. we've spoken on the phone, and I'll be preparing you for court today." She holds out her hand, and I take it. She's pretty. I'd say mid-twenties with mousy brown hair and hazel eyes. Her frame is small, but her handshake is strong. I respect a strong handshake.

"Good morning, Candace. Please, call me Ed."

We sit and go through the first day of the trial. We're looking at multiple days for now, and then it'll be up to the jury to decide whether it's guilty or not guilty. That statement alone fills me with rage. Strangers get to hear his pleas, he will get a chance to charm them, and these people will ultimately decide whether my brother is punished or not. I mentally push the rage down; I need the numbness to take over during the trial.

Today will be opening statements and laying the land. Tomorrow will be the start of the prosecution's evidence. My parents have decided not to come to court. My mum can't cope with any more heartbreak, let alone hearing what her son has done in detail.

Candace leaves me alone again, and I make myself a coffee as I wait to be called in. My mind wanders to Noel. What's he thinking at this moment? Does he feel anything? Guilt and remorse would be too hopeful to expect from him. He is a grade-A sociopath. Of course, I've known this since I was a small child. No one else has seen it other than his victims. My mind shifts to Kiera. How is she holding up? She's been strong, not only for herself and my parents but for me. She's supporting me through this, and it's something I haven't had before. Pure support, no ulterior motive, no power plays, just her being her.

My numbness thaws for a millisecond, allowing me to feel love before there's a knock at the door and I'm called into court.

———

"THE DEFENDANT PLEADS NOT GUILTY TO ALL COUNTS on account of Anosognosia and Bipolar Disorder."

Bullshit. There's nothing wrong with him other than him being a psychopath. Pathetic that he's muddying these disorders with his lies.

"The defendant feels greatly for the victims of his previous actions…"

Bull. Shit.

"The defendant does not wish harm on any living being…"

Lies.

The fury bubbles from my toes to my brain like lava bubbling over the top of a volcano that is waiting to erupt. He's pleading he has a mental illness. We all know that's bullshit. I want nothing more than to drive something sharp into his skull. Noel is sitting there with a small, almost undetectable, smug smile on his face whilst his lawyer speaks. I see it, though, especially when he turns around to see Kiera and I sitting behind him. With his face away from the judge and jury, he has the audacity to wink.

The rage…

Chapter Forty-Two

KIERA

This is weird. It's day one of the trial, and although I know what Noel did to Ed growing up and his pathetic attempt to bully me, hearing what he's done to countless other women is truly sickening.

"He…he told me I was worthless. He told me I was too broken to be loved. Th-this was after he broke my ribs and kept me locked…" One woman broke down on the stand to the point she had to be carried off by a gentle guard. Noel really did break her.

"He isolated me from my friends and family." This one is braver. She stared straight into his eyes and said, "He beat me so badly I had to have an emergency hysterectomy. It's only by luck I was taken to the hospital. He went out, and I walked out of my house and to my neighbours. I was eight weeks pregnant with his child. Now, I'll never get to experience growing a human inside me."

My tears sting as they roll down my cheeks. Ten women, Ed and myself are all testifying against him. There are statements from a dozen more, but they couldn't face coming to court. From what I've heard in the statements, I'm surprised they're still standing. He didn't just physically abuse them. He mentally controlled and beat down these women. One is currently in a mental health facility. She's been in there for three years trying to repair herself after having Noel in her life.

There's no way in hell the jury can consider him not guilty. No way.

TODAY HAS BEEN DRAINING. ED AND I HAVE BEEN silent since getting home, both taking really long, hot showers and then slumping on the sofa. With zero energy to speak of, we order in paninis from the late-night café and try to summon the energy to eat when they arrive.

It's nine in the evening, and my nerves are racing. Tomorrow, both of us will testify, and then we'll have to listen to the defence team. It is going to suck big hairy balls. I glance over at Ed, who's staring into space. His body is practically vibrating with negative energy. We haven't spoken since we got home at seven; we've just been in our own heads.

I reach over and grab his hand, which is ice cold. He's normally hotter than Satan's armpit, and now,

I'm worried. "Ed?" I gently run my thumb over his knuckles as he slowly turns his head towards me. His eyes are devoid of emotion. After a moment, he shakes his head and smiles. His hand gradually warms, as does the affection in his eyes, almost as if his thoughts were blocking any form of warmth from him.

"Hey." His devastating smile is missing today, but that's completely understandable. Instead, I'm greeted with a small smile that does not reach his eyes.

I pull him towards me and lay his head on my lap, running my fingers through his hair.

"Today was tough." I smile. Even though he can't see it, I'm hoping he feels it.

"Tomorrow is going to be worse." His body stiffens again, and I curl mine around his top half and hold him.

"Don't push me out," I whisper. He sighs at my words and wraps his arms around mine, holding me in place. My back is starting to scream at me, but he needs comfort, and honestly, so do I.

Ed rolls onto his back, his head still nestled in my lap as I stroke his soft brown hair. "I don't mean to. I've spent years dealing with stuff on my own, and I've forgotten how to open up properly." He sighs heavily as he fiddles with the promise ring on my left hand, which is resting on his chest. "I don't know how I feel about the trial. I feel like I should feel guilty testifying against my only brother, but the pain he's caused me and others…" Ed stares off into the distance, the war in his eyes evident by the furrow in his brow getting deeper.

"You couldn't have known what he was going to

turn into or how many other people he was going to hurt, but you are taking a step towards saving others from his torture."

Ed shifts his eyes to mine and holds my gaze. There's a subtle change in them. Almost as if he's starting to believe what he's doing is right, even though he may feel guilty.

"Let's go to bed. We've got more of this hell coming up, but it'll be over soon." We rise from the sofa, head to our room and fall into our bed. I'm out within minutes, but I have no doubt Ed takes longer to go to sleep.

We are going through the motions when we get up. Shower, dress, breakfast, coffee, out the door. We sit in the courtroom, waiting to be called to the stand.

"The next witness to be called is Kiera Cole." My time is here, and I refuse to avoid Noel's smug face. He's acting as if he's here for his enjoyment and acts as if he won't be punished for his crimes.

The light I normally carry with me is being shrouded by dark thoughts. I want him to suffer just like he made Ed and his other victims suffer. I want him to go to jail, and I want the other inmates to make his life utter hell so that he can't sleep and wonders what's going to happen when the lights go out, wonders whether he'll live another day or die in prison. The alarming strength those thoughts give me allows me to straighten my spine as I place my hand on the bible and swear to tell the truth and nothing but the truth.

My last thought before the prosecution team asks

their questions as I stare into those dead eyes of his is I hope he gets everything he deserves. Terror, pain, nightmares… I hope he rots in prison for the rest of his life.

"Miss Cole…" And it begins.

Chapter Forty-Three

ED

I sit in the row of seats at the back of the courtroom, my bum getting numb from the wood. It's honestly worse than a church pew. But as I sit, I watch Kiera on the stand, her back straight, her voice confident as she retells the events of the night Noel attacked her. She stares straight into his eyes at one point, and honest to God, if I hadn't been watching his reaction, I would have missed the millisecond he slumped slightly as she recalled him dressing her in what he thought was sexy lingerie in her own words. "It's clear that even through his attempts to dominate and intimidate me, this man has no idea what to do with a woman."

I have to hide the smile that tugs at my mouth. She is attacking his manhood, possibly to provoke a reaction from him that the jury would see, but in reality, I think it's because she was angry that he managed to take advantage of her. Twice. I feel nothing but pride as I sit and listen to Kiera's testimony. She may not act like she went through a lot, but she did, and once this trial is over, I'm going to whisk us away for a week or two to relax and recover.

After Kiera finishes her testimony, we recess. I meet her outside the courthouse, and we walk to the nearest Starbucks. Luckily, you can't go for long in London without a Starbucks popping up. Kiera needs a large cup of her "happy juice," and although I could quite happily knock back a whiskey right now, a coffee will have to do.

"How are you feeling?" she asks as the aroma of coffee envelopes my senses.

"I don't know. It's like I'm watching a movie rather than actually watching it happen, if that makes sense."

She nods thoughtfully as I think about testifying this afternoon.

"It does, but we've got this. He'll be punished for what he's done." Before I can answer, the barista calls her name and hands over our coffees. Kiera's looks like it should come with a health and safety warning. Honestly, it's the size of a bucket.

We have over forty minutes before we're due back, so we sit on a bench near the courtroom to eat our homemade sandwiches and drink our coffee. For January, it's not actually that cold. The sun is shining through the bare trees, and it's a heady 12 degrees today with no wind, so it feels quite warm in the winter sun.

We sit, watching the people of the city go about their days, and Kiera lays her head on my shoulder. "It'll turn out the way it's meant to. I can hear your gears whirring away in there." She speaks softly whilst sipping her latte. She's not wrong. My head is trying to find the logical conclusion to all of this by running through various scenarios. It's the analyst in me, I suppose. I try to turn my head off, even if it's just whilst we're here sitting on a wooden bench next to a path with tree branches hanging over us.

A big sigh comes through my nose as I force my muscles and mind to relax, and Kiera snuggles her head further as if feeling me relax beneath her. For the moment, I do feel calmer, and then our alarm goes off, telling us it's time to return to the courtroom and prepare for the afternoon. My shoulders are tense, and you could probably build a solid housing foundation on them.

"MR GREEN, YOU ALLEGE YOU WERE ABUSED FROM A young age by your brother?"

"You allege you couldn't tell your parents. Did you think they wouldn't believe you? Why do you think that is?"

"You haven't spoken to your brother in years, and when you saw him at family events, you didn't talk to each other. However, once you did speak to him again, he was arrested later that day. Was this planned?"

Noel's defence team is on fire, clutching at straws, but on fire. Luckily, the prosecution is better. They knew the questions that would be asked, so they asked the same ones in a different way to show who Noel truly was. But he sits there, during my time on the stand, smirking at me like he did when we were kids. Almost as if he knew he couldn't be caught.

The thing is, he has been caught, and I can't see how the jury could find him anything other than guilty. We have lots of witness statements, solid testimonies, but there's something niggling at me deep down. What if he doesn't get punished for his actions? What are the implications for those who testified against him?

I stand in the wooden box, retelling my story, knowing I should show emotion, but I can't. I will not show him any more weakness than I already have. He took my childhood, he tried to destroy the happiness I've found with Kiera, and he's taken so much from other people that I cannot show weakness now.

After my testimony, the judge calls it a day, and we head home for the evening. Both Kiera and I are quiet on our journey. We're both mentally exhausted from the day. Once we're in, Kiera heads over to the shower as I heat up some microwave meals. I honestly can't be bothered to cook a proper meal right now. I have my shower after Kiera, and we flop down on the sofa with our sad-looking meals. Why do they never look like the pictures?

"I didn't realise how draining court would be," Kiera says quietly as she stares at a spot on the wall in the living room.

"I know. I'm sorry you got dragged into this." I shake my head. If we hadn't gone to that family day, they wouldn't have met, and his slimy paws wouldn't have touched her. I regret they ever met, but I also know without that event, he wouldn't have been caught, and all of these people would have stayed silent about their trauma.

"Don't be daft. I'd rather go through this shit a thousand times than never having a minute with you." Damn. Shots fired straight to my bloody heart.

I squeeze her hard, not knowing what on earth I can say back. I'm thankful we found each other. I'm thankful she lets me love her. I'm thankful that, amongst all of the other feelings, she's managed to mend my broken pieces and glue them together.

Chapter Forty-Four

KIERA

I t's the last day of the trial, and honestly, I cannot wait for this to end. It's exhausting, not only giving evidence but listening to all of the other testimonies and hearing the defence team trying to make Noel sound like a decent human being.

We sit in the stands today, listening to the prosecution and defence give their closing statements. Our side did a damn good job, but if I wasn't personally involved in this trial and I sat in the jurors' place, I have to admit the defence team have given an equally good showing. I pay attention to what both teams have to say, watching the jurors and hoping they find him guilty. He is guilty!

Ed places his hand on my knee, and it's then I notice how nervous I am. My leg has been bouncing more than a four-year-old on blue smarties. I need to calm down, or I'll wind Ed up, too, which won't be helpful. He's already strung tightly, and I fear he's going to snap.

Ed squeezes my knee, and I slide my hand into his and squeeze back. I can feel how tense he is next to me as the statements come to a close. I know he's going through hell mentally, and I'm not sure what I can do to help. I snap out of my head when I hear the judge sum up the trial. The jurors have been asked to head to their room. Now, we wait.

THE JURORS HAVE BEEN IN THEIR ROOM FOR THREE hours already. We've been out for coffee and lunch, nervously glancing at our phones to make sure we don't miss any notifications to head back to the court-room. It's two in the afternoon, and Ed's nervous energy is radiating from him.

I'm glancing in a shop window with the hope of distracting myself. What's taking them so long to decide? Surely, it's an open-and-shut case? Noel is guilty. It's been proven with a mountain of evidence. As I'm pointing out a beautiful art piece to Ed, his phone rings.

"Okay, thanks for letting me know." He hangs up, and his face is unreadable.

"What's happening?"

"The jury has made their decision. We're due back in court." Ed's tone is clipped, and although I know he's not aiming his frustration at me, it still hurts.

We rush back to court. Ed is slightly in front of me as I struggle to keep his pace.

"Ed, slow down a little." I am breathless as I practically trot to keep up with him.

"Let's get this over with." He walks faster as we near the courthouse, almost running up the steps.

By the time we sit in the stands again, his body is tense, and his hands are clasped in his lap whilst I sound asthmatic and attempt to get my breathing under control. The lead juror stands when the judge invites them to do so.

"After reviewing the evidence thoroughly, the jury has reached a decision. We find the defendant guilty of...." My ears are ringing with a high-pitched noise as the juror goes through the crimes they've found Noel guilty of. I glance at Ed, who's sitting just as tense as when we came back into the courtroom. Why doesn't he look happy?

After the juror sits down, the judge sentences Noel to ten years in prison. We stand when the judge exits and watch as Noel is taken away. The smug smile he wore during the trial is no longer there. He is now wearing an expression of shock and disbelief. The courtroom empties as Ed sits, staring at the spot where Noel sat. I gently place my hand over his clasped ones.

"Ed?" I say as gently as I can. I don't know where his head is at. He turns to me, and his eyes are devoid of all emotion. His body is still tense and stiff when he looks down at my hand covering his. He stands without warning but as if in slow motion.

"Let's go home," he says flatly.

We travel home in silence, unlike the previous days where it was through exhaustion, this trip feels awkward. I don't know where his head is at, and he has not looked at me since we left the courtroom. I curl into myself on the train and scroll through my phone. I text Jess the verdict, and she's thrilled for us. I don't share the current energy radiating from Ed, mainly because I don't understand it.

We get home, and Ed heads straight for the shower. I stand in the open front door with a feeling in the pit of my stomach. I can't describe it, but all I feel at this moment is unsettled. I close the door, dump my coat and bag on the sofa and head into the kitchen to make a cuppa. It's nearly dinner time, and I'm not hungry yet, but I know I will be later. I fumble through the cupboards mindlessly, not really seeing what's in front of me. Sod it, we'll order in when we're hungry.

When Ed finally comes back into the kitchen, he doesn't appear any more relaxed. His hair is still wet from the shower, making it look floppy. If it wasn't for the stoic expression on his face, I'd be jumping into his arms right now. We should be celebrating. It feels like it has been too long since we were intimate, and I miss him.

I finish making my coffee when I feel him come closer. His body heat is at my back as his hands reach for the countertop, his arms caging me in. Ed's lips touch my neck, which normally leaves me a melting puddle of horny, but today, it feels different. I turn in his arms to try and read his face. No emotion. My spidey senses are tingling, and although he's meeting my gaze, his eyes are sending shivers down my spine, and not in a good way.

Chapter Forty-Five

ED

I feel numb. There's nothing in me at all. I should feel elated, relieved…something! But I feel nothing. Whilst I was in the shower, I wanted to feel the hot water fall down my body and release this tension, but I was devoid of feeling. The one thing that makes me feel is Kiera. Maybe being close to her will help me or at least unlock something so I can process the last few days.

I find her in the kitchen, and although my mind is telling me I want her, I want to feel her beneath me, that I need to feel her, I still feel numb. I crowd her in the hopes her scent breeches whatever blockade is in my body and mind. She turns in my arms and stares at me. She looks wary, but maybe she's just tired like I am.

I back up a little and hold out my hand to her. She glances from my hand back into my eyes and takes it. I sense a little hesitation, but I grab her hand and drag her to the bedroom. The need for her is taking over me. I need to feel again, and she's my key. Kiera doesn't say anything as I sit her on the bed and remove her top. Pushing her back, I make quick work of removing her trousers and look at her. She really is beautiful.

Hovering over her, I kiss her neck, letting myself pause for a moment to feel her pulse beneath my lips. It flutters as I gently graze my fingertips across her stomach. My mind isn't really in focus as I'm moving across her body. I'm mentally fighting to take in her curves, soft skin and smell, but my body is moving on autopilot. The raw memories of court are flying through my head as I try to shake them off. Who thinks of that when they're in the middle of foreplay?

The swirling torment of thoughts is scrambling around in my brain. I need to stop them and focus on Kiera. I want to focus on Kiera! I hear her voice through the images in the courtroom. I see Noel's face smirking at me as I speak on the stand, and the anger that rolls through me feels like a dam that's about to burst. I can feel Kiera around me, calming the torrent inside me.

Focus, Ed!

When I do manage to focus again, Kiera is face down, and I'm holding her arms behind her back, thrusting into her. How did we get here? Why don't I remember teasing her? Has she come? I'm struggling to gain control over my mind and body. I notice a tear making its way down Kiera's nose, and it's then I realise I'm coming. What has come over me? This has never happened before.

I remove myself from her and almost run into the bathroom. That's not okay! What the hell just happened? I feel like I'm losing control. I stand in the shower and turn it on. The icy blast of water thrums over me before it warms, but my mind is still trying to piece together the last however long it was we were in the bedroom. Sinking down, I hug my knees, feeling the coldness of the tiles against my back and the shower tray beneath me.

It takes me a moment to realise tears are streaming down my face. Years of repressed anger, fear and help-lessness all come out as I sit here. After what feels like hours, although it is likely minutes, I stand and shut off the water.

I need help. That much is evident.

I open the bathroom door and head back into the bedroom, towelling down as I go. I'm searching for my phone. I need to contact my therapist, and I notice Kiera isn't in here. Wrapping the towel around my waist, I walk into the living room and can't see her there or in the kitchen. Panic rips through me with a fresh wave of emotion and pain.

I grab my phone from the kitchen island and make a call.

"Dr Gordon's office. How may I help you?"

"Hi there. I need to see Dr Gordon urgently. It's Edward Green."

"Hello, Mr Green. Bear with me whilst I check his calendar."

"Hi, I've got a video call appointment available in an hour if that suits you?"

"Excellent, thank you."

With that taken care of, I go through my messages and find one from Kiera.

> Kiera: Gone to Mum and Dad's for the night. Not running, but need space.

A lump forms in my throat as I respond. I want to apologise for how badly I've fucked up. I want to tell her to come back and never leave me. I want to beg for forgiveness, but instead, I send a simple apology.

> Me: I'm so sorry. I have no idea what happened. I'm seeing Dr Gordon in an hour. Will I see you tomorrow?

I really hope I haven't fucked this up.

Chapter Forty-Six

ED

D r Gordon is scribbling down notes frantically after I tell him about the last few months. I haven't seen him since Kiera moved in, and there's no reason for that other than I felt happy and content in life.

"I believe you've experienced something called a rage blackout."

"What is that? I've never had that happen before." I'm staring at the screen, hoping for a magical cure for whatever this is.

"A rage blackout is a period of intense anger during which a person may lose awareness or memory of their actions. It may also result in them potentially harming themselves or others."

My mind spirals. That definitely sounds like what happened. I don't remember anything during my "blackout," and I'm ninety per cent sure I hurt Kiera.

Maybe not physically, but I'm certain I did emotionally.

"I've been angrier than that before, and it's never happened. Why now?"

"Ed, you've suppressed a lot of emotions over the years. Yes, you may have had bouts of anger, but they haven't been deep-rooted like your feelings towards your brother. With the attacks on Kiera and the court appearance, there's a lot going on to make those feelings 'erupt like lava,' as you put it."

"I think I hurt her. During the blackout. I ran into the bathroom after I finally managed to focus on the present, and when I came out, she was gone."

Scribbling again. Dr Gordon has brilliant reviews and is the one therapist I feel comfortable with. He doesn't have that "I'm judging you" expression on his face whilst he's talking to you. As he concentrates, I take in his features. He sits at his desk in his office. He has a full head of white hair, and his skin is darker than when I last saw him. Maybe he was on holiday. I don't peg him as a sunbed or fake tan kind of person. His thin, black wire-rim glasses are perched on his straight nose, and there's a crease between his brows as he jots down his notes. When he looks up, I can see his pale grey eyes looking at me. It's almost as if there isn't a screen in between us.

"Ed, I'd like to talk further about the events that led up to you potentially hurting Kiera."

That, right there, those few words fill me with dread. Yes, of course, I want to get better so this shit doesn't happen again, but I also fear delving deeper inside my head. What else has been locked up waiting to come out?

MY HEAD IS SPLITTING. I REACH UP TO THE TOP SHELF for my headache tablets as the coffee machine whirrs its happy tune, and the smell of strong coffee hits my senses. I spent three hours with Dr Gordon. He had to reschedule someone, and I feel awful, but I also feel like we've gone through a lot today, and although I want to sleep for a week right now, I do feel a little better. We've scheduled a two-hour slot twice a week for the next month to see how I get on. Even though this time wasn't dangerous, we can't be certain next time won't be…if there is a next time.

I want to tell Kiera. She's been the first person who pops into my head when something funny, sad or slightly inconvenient happens to me. I have to tell her, but does she want to listen? Will she pick up the phone? I knock back my tablets with an iced water and head to the sofa. Picking up my phone, I zero in on the name amongst the many notifications on there.

Kiera.

I open up her message and see that it's a long one. I settle down and read it.

> Kiera: Hey Ed. It's been a few hours, and I haven't heard from you. I wanted to check in to see if you're ok. I don't know what happened, but you weren't there today. You were different, and you hurt me. Physically and emotionally. But I know it wasn't you. Mum and Dad are going away for a few days, so I'm going to stay here until Thursday to house-sit. I just need a little space and rest. It's been exhausting for both of us, and I don't doubt you could use the space too. Remember that I love you. xxx

I'm crying again. I hurt her. I want to know where so I can make sure she heals, but I don't know whether I should call or not. This is excruciating and something I haven't encountered before. But then, this is my first long-term relationship. I don't want to lose her. What do I respond with?

Before I know what's happening, I have two fingers of Scotch in a glass, and I feel the burn in my throat. This isn't a healthy way to process, but my mind clearly doesn't give a fuck as I gulp and pour another glass. I should have eaten today. My head is a little wobbly, and I can feel the darkness pulling me in. Downing my third glass, I text her back.

> Me: You deserve better, maybe we reconsider our relationship.

I slink onto the sofa. The coldness sweeps over me

as the Scotch feebly attempts to warm me up from the inside. I toss my phone down and stare out of the window. Not bothering with a glass any longer, I swig out of the bottle.

Well, shit.

Chapter Forty-Seven

KIERA

I'm on the train, heading to Mum and Dad's. I'm not running. Well, maybe I am, but not properly. Ed scared the crap out of me, and instead of facing it like an adult, I run to my parents, not that they know why I'm randomly popping round.

It was the look in his eyes and the way he took me. I couldn't see the spark and love that's normally shining in Ed's eyes. It was like they were completely vacant of anything as if his body took over and there was nothing behind his eyes at all. It honestly scared me. I know I should have stayed to talk to him, but I couldn't. I needed a minute to myself to process what happened.

The train rolls to a stop, and I walk the ten minutes to Mum and Dad's. I'm going to enjoy a night at theirs to relax and hopefully switch my brain off. I also need to keep a poker face so Mum doesn't read me like a book because the last thing I need is to explain what transpired. I have the soothing tones of Iron Maiden rocking through my earphones as I near my parents' house. The guitar strokes are calming my mood from earlier and easing the thoughts in my mind. I'm really looking forward to whatever Mum makes for dinner and a chilled evening.

I enter and take note of the chaos in front of me. Bags are everywhere in the hallway, and clothes are piled high on the dining table. I can hear Mum shouting instructions to Dad, who mumbles something in return. The worst part? I can't smell anything cooking.

"Mum? Dad? You being robbed?" I kick off my trainers and shrug my coat off. I'd hang it on the back of a chair, but there's no space. What are they doing?

I turn to see my flustered mum carrying shampoo and conditioner to dump onto what was the dining table.

"Kiera!" Bottles dismissed into the pile of clothes, she flings her arms around me. Nothing can beat a mum hug.

"What you doing?" I swing my arms open to gesture at the mess.

"Oh, we decided to go away for a couple of days. I started packing, which led to sorting out the wardrobe. Well, you know how your dad never throws anything away. Then I couldn't find the hold-all bags, so I sent your dad into the loft, where he found four bags of clothes. Can you imagine? So we've been sorting and packing and landed in a mess. I know you've come to stay for the night, but we're heading out early in the morning to miss the traffic."

I take a breath. Mum can be chaotic, and I'm sure there's some ADHD in there when she starts organising. It's never quick and easy, bless her. I start to fold clothes on the table whilst she whittles on about wanting some fresh air, so they have booked a cabin in the woods with no internet or phone signal. *Can't see anything going wrong there at all.*

Mum and I are chatting whilst I sort out her clutter, and we pile everything that's going to charity in bags ready for them to take when they get back from their trip. Their cases are now packed, and I sit with a cuppa, scrolling through the local takeaways because I'm apparently eating alone as they're heading to bed early.

"Now, love, if you need to stay for a couple days, you're welcome to. The house will be yours to use. You do look like you could do with some quiet time." Damn her knowing shit without knowing.

"Thanks, Mum. I appreciate it. I might stay a couple of nights." That slipped out. I didn't plan on staying longer than tonight, but I could do with some alone time. A lot has cracked on this year.

I fire off a text to Ed to let him know I'm staying to house-sit. It's not entirely the truth, but it'll do for now, and then I order myself a pizza for dinner. Mum and Dad head off to bed, and I run myself a nice hot bath. I've got plenty of time to prune up before the pizza gets here. I leave my phone in the bedroom and relax. I have candles, a face mask and music playing on Alexa.

When I dip my foot into the bath, I get the hot tingles and smile. It's weird, but I love that burning-tingling sensation when a bath is too hot.

The steam filling the air is comforting, and I lie back to enjoy my relaxation playlist. It's mainly rock, but it relaxes me more than the plinky plonky music you hear in spas. I must have drifted off because before I know it, my timer is going off, and the bath is a little cooler than when I got in. Stepping out, I head to my room to get changed into my PJs. The pizza will be here in ten, and I can't wait to dive into that greasy mess with a glass of wine.

I pick up my phone as I head downstairs and look at my notifications. I stop mid-staircase when I see a message from Ed.

> Ed: You deserve better, maybe we reconsider our relationship.

You can pack that shit in!
Absolutely not! He is not breaking up with me because we've had a rough time. I storm into the kitchen and pour myself a nice glass of white Italian. Taking deep breaths, I decide to wait for my pizza before responding. I'm going to need some carbs.

Just as I take a sip of my crisp wine, the doorbell rings. One thing that will never let you down emotionally is food. I thank the driver and head to the kitchen. Two slices in is when I decide to call Ed. It rings out the first time I call. *That shithead better not be avoiding me!*

Four times, Ed's phone rings out, and I'm stress-eating this pizza into oblivion. Stupid ass man. I check the time, and it's now late in the evening. There's nothing I can do now. By the time I got home, it would be too late to talk, and I'm two glasses of wine in. Let alone, if he's had anything to drink...we won't be making any headway tonight.

Change of plans. I'm going to finish this pizza and bottle of wine, sleep it off, and tomorrow, I'm going home to sort this shit out. He thinks I deserve better? We are each other's other half—as Hallmark as that sounds, I don't want anyone else. We all have baggage, and he's going to strap on a pair and have this conversation rather than sending me a shitty text.

I flop down on the sofa to finish my wine now that the pizza is gone. I grab a pen and paper to write down the events that have happened over the last few months. Lists are how I process. And wine!

Chapter Forty-Eight

ED

Ow! My head hurts. Why does my body ache, too? My eyes are screaming at me as I try to open them, but the light is blinding when I eventually crack them open. The view in front of me is scrambling my brain, though. I appear to be on the floor, looking under the sofa, but I don't know how or why. When I attempt to move, my leg falls with a thud. Ah! That explains the strange view; my leg and half my body were still on the sofa. No wonder my body aches. There's no telling how long my dumb ass has been sleeping like this.

I tear myself off the floor with grunts and groans and notice the empty bottle of Scotch. Yes, that makes much more sense as the events of last night come crashing back into my mind. Shit! I sent a message to Kiera. I scramble around, trying to find my phone. It's not in a logical place, which means I launched it somewhere. After twenty minutes, I find it and plug it in to charge, make a coffee, and then head to the bathroom for a hot shower to chase the haze surrounding my mind.

After, I dress in comfy clothes and feel full of regret. Not just from the drinking but the series of mood swings that led up to yesterday. I regret sending Kiera that message. She does deserve better than me, but I can't imagine my life without her. Heading into the kitchen, my coffee is now at the perfect temperature to drink, and I look at my phone. Four missed calls from Kiera last night, then nothing. Fuck, fuck, fuck. It's ten in the morning; she should be up. I can call her. I should call her.

I dial, and it goes straight to voicemail. Shit! I leave my phone on the counter and make another coffee. It's going to take a few of those to chase away the last of the hangover. I also need to eat. Did I have dinner last night? I look through the cupboard, waiting for inspiration to hit me about what to eat that would soak up the rest of last night when I hear a key in the lock. My back straightens as I go to the door. No one else has a key except...

Kiera.

She enters with puffy eyes and a look of pure rage on her face. She is so angry she can defeat Voldemort without any magic. When her gaze lands on me, I freeze. That's when I noticed I'd backed away from the door. Kiera takes me in, her face softening ever so slightly before she barrels into me and whacks my arm hard before pacing around the apartment. I'm sure something has been fractured.

"What the—"

"Don't you even start with me! How DARE YOU try to break up with me over text! You spineless twat waffle!" Tears are threatening to spill from her eyes, but I can't help but laugh. This makes her even more furious. She advances on me with an expression that could make milk curdle. I hold my hands up in surrender, but she doesn't back down.

Dropping the bags I hadn't noticed she was carrying, she hits my arms again and again. Each blow is less devastating than the last until I wrap her in my arms. I have no right to hug her because she's right. Twat waffle still makes me laugh, but she's right. I am spineless, but I also don't want to break up with her. I feel Kiera's forehead press against my chest, and I rest my chin on top of her head.

"I'm sorry. I am spineless, but I don't want to break up. I...spiralled and drank too much, and it's no excuse, but—"

"You're a dick, Ed." Those gorgeous blue eyes blink up at me. The threatening tears have retreated, and so has most of her anger. Most.

"I am. But I'm your dick."

She allows me to hold her for a few more moments before she backs up. Kiera stares at me with those ocean blues, baring her soul. So beautiful. "Make me a coffee, shithead, then we'll talk."

Kiera shrugs off her coat and shoes and makes her way to the sofa.

I head over to the kitchen and make us a coffee. Then we'll talk.

Chapter Forty-Nine

KIERA

My initial fury that got my ass up, out of bed, showered and back home so early after a bottle of wine has dissipated a little. Ed looks like crap, and it makes me feel better knowing he doesn't want to break up. I'll allow my inner Hulk to return to good old Bruce for now.

I sit on the sofa, waiting for my coffee. I rushed out of my parents' house this morning, wanting to sort this out. I know Ed has suffered in the past, and spiralling wasn't the healthiest way to deal with it, but I also know he wouldn't have been able to stop it.

Ed brings me my coffee with a small smile and sits at the other end of the sofa. I feel the familiar tingles the hot coffee cup brings to my fingertips and wait for him to say something. It becomes evident, though, that he isn't going to start.

"So, we gonna talk about why you suddenly think I can do better?" My voice is more clipped and sterner than I intend, but it sparks a reaction out of him.

His smile fades into a frown, and he stares down into his cup as if he's expecting an answer to jump out of it. "Kiera, I…" He drags his eyes from his cup to meet my expectant gaze. I have a feeling his text was a flippant response to his drinking and mood, but it hurt like hell.

"I didn't mean it. Well, I did…but I didn't. I've been in a bad place, and you left. I hurt you, and you deserve so much better than that. What we were—"

"Were? So you're actually trying to break up with me? You think I didn't realise you weren't there yesterday? You were somewhere else, and the lights weren't on in your eyes, Ed. I'm not fucking stupid, so don't treat me like a little girl who doesn't know what's going on."

His eyes widen. My anger is back and isn't simmering like it did when I walked in. I love him, but my God, I want to staple something to his head right now for being an idiot. Putting his coffee down on the table, he drops his head in his hands and shakes it from side to side. I want to comfort him, but he needs to tell me what he wants. I don't want this to end, but it won't work if both of us aren't in it.

"What happened, Ed?" I keep my voice soft this time. I want to understand what happened, where he went, and what snapped in his head.

After a few moments, he releases his head and looks at me with such sadness in his eyes." I wanted to feel. You make me feel. I wanted to get rid of the anxiety and anger. I don't know what happened. I spoke with Dr Gordon after you left. He said it was a rage blackout. When I came out of the darkness, I ran to the bathroom. I knew I'd hurt you and hated it. I hated myself. When I finally emerged, you'd gone," Ed says quietly, and I'm straining to hear him.

I remain silent, waiting for him to continue, hoping this isn't the end for us.

"When you left, I called the doctor for an emergency appointment. I hadn't dealt with a lot of my feelings towards Noel because after I met you, I was happy. I thought they'd gone. But they were still there. With the trial, all those feelings exploded and sent me into a rage blackout. I have no idea how we got to the bedroom. I have no memory of that timeframe, and I'm still not sure how long I lost…"

"An hour. You lost an hour." My eyes can't quite meet his, but I see them out of my peripheral. I feel the emotions radiating off of him, and if my gaze meets his, I will cry.

"Shit. I'm so sorry." His eyes are watering, and I know mine are going to be next. I need to divert my attention so I don't cry, not yet, anyway.

"After your session with the doc, you decided to empty a bottle of Scotch and break up with me? How did that fit in with your session?"

"It didn't. I spiralled. I thought I didn't deserve you, and you…Kiera, you deserve the fucking world." On those last two words, he looks at me with such conviction. I think I'm starting to understand.

"So, basically, you were lost in another dimension

for an hour, sent there by your rage, and when you came back home and realised you'd hurt me. I ran, and that sent you into a spiral of despair, and you think you're not good enough for me." I offer a small smile. I don't want to make light of the situation, but I do want us to lighten up a little.

Ed offers a weak laugh. "In a nutshell, love. Yeah, that's about it."

"Well, Mr Bossy Pants, you don't get to tell me I deserve better. I love YOU, and WE will get through this together." I reach over and hold his hand. My insides warm when he squeezes mine back. "Oh, and maybe more sessions with the doc and less Scotch for a while?" I squeal as he suddenly pulls me onto him and hugs me tightly. My lungs feel like they're about to burst.

"I fucking love you, Kiera." Our faces are touching whilst we embrace, and I can feel my cheek dampening, but it's not my tears this time.

"I fucking love you, too, Ed."

Chapter Fifty

ED

I 'm so bloody stupid. My self-destructive behaviour nearly pushed her away. I'm lucky that she's as stubborn as a goat. We spend hours talking about my past, the trial, therapy, how we can move forward, and most importantly, how we are a team and *nothing* will get between us.

We talk in-depth about the rage blackout and do some research. I tell Kiera that I'll be continuing with Dr Gordon weekly regardless of how happy I feel. There are a lot of deep-rooted feelings that need to be dealt with rather than hiding them in the shadows, waiting to drag me down, and she wholeheartedly agrees that this is the best action for not only me but us.

The cloud that has been hanging over me, shrouding my happy thoughts and allowing the darkness to take over, has been sent back into the shadows thanks to Kiera's light. Her light has always been there, but I haven't been letting it in lately, and the warmth from it is freeing. I feel like I can breathe for the first time in months.

It's nearing lunchtime, and I hear Kiera's stomach starting to protest. Did she skip breakfast to be here this morning? I do appreciate her wanting to fix this, but I also know a hangry Kiera isn't good for anyone. I haven't had a chance to shop, so I order her favourite lunch and make us a cuppa to tide her over until it arrives.

Kiera comes up behind me and slides her arms around my waist. The warmth from her touch is exhilarating when I've felt nothing but numbness for a while. I lean into her as I finish our coffees and spin in her arms. Leaning down, I kiss her. Kiera's arms reach around my neck as I snake one arm around her waist, and my other hand grasps her hair. I touch her lips lightly with mine, and Kiera opens her mouth, letting me in, deepening the kiss. I kiss her fiercely, and we moan into each other's mouths. God, I've missed her.

My arm skims her waist, hip, and then I grab her ass. Its roundness fits perfectly in my hand as I squeeze her, which makes her giggle against my lips. Kiera hooks her legs around my waist when I lift her, deepening our kiss further. If I run out of air, I'll die a happy man.

I carry Kiera to the bedroom and lay her on the bed as I fall on top of her. She places her hands on either side of my face, looking deep into my eyes, and I can tell she's making sure it's me here and not a blackout.

"I'm here, baby," I say, leaning in to kiss her. She hooks her hands behind my neck, pulling me in deeper. I can feel myself hardening against her, and she rocks against my length.

I push my hips into her, my hands roaming over her body. I feel like a teenager again with how desperate I am to touch her. Kiera rips at my clothes as I do hers. It feels like it's once again our first time together. Tearing off her clothes, I devour her skin with my lips, tongue, and teeth. Kiera's hands tangle in my hair as my mouth travels down, lapping up every sweet inch of her skin. Hooking my thumbs in her knickers, I slide them slowly down her legs.

"Ed, come the fuck on. I need you now!"

I laugh as I toss her knickers behind me and place my fingers in her slit to feel how ready she is for me. Sopping!

I hurry my boxers off and ready myself at her entrance. I slick the tip of my cock, rubbing myself up and down to tease her, and Kiera bucks against me before dragging me down on top of her. I kiss her deeply before sitting back on my heels, bringing Kiera with me, and she slams down on me, eyes rolling in the back of her head as she moans. Steading herself with her hands on my shoulders, she rides me hard and fast. Neither of us is going to last long at this rate. Leaning back slightly, I can feel her clench around me. I use my thumb on her clit, bringing her to climax so hard that I think my cock may break under the pressure.

I tip my head back, releasing a growl from the depths of my body. Damn, I can feel everything inside of her, and the tingling at the base of my spine is starting. I want this to last longer, but my God, she's rocking on me, and the orgasm that's building is going to shatter my soul. Kiera's nails dig into my shoulders as she adjusts her angle slightly and comes again. This time, when her body squeezes me, I come and can see the universe behind my eyes as her name explodes from my lips. My soul officially shatters.

I fall back, and Kiera collapses on top of me, both of us breathless. I need a minute for my vision to return to normal. It wasn't the longest I've lasted by a long shot, but my God, it was powerful.

As we both come down from the highs we've encountered, we still can't move. Both of us lie there in bliss. Then the door buzzer sounds. I'd completely forgotten I'd ordered lunch. Impeccable timing, though. I scramble to chuck some clothes on and open the door to receive our goodies. Kiera strolls into the kitchen wearing just a t-shirt and underwear and looking incredibly sexy with her hair ruffled and a sated expression on her face.

We sit and eat our breakfast torpedos, although now nearer lunchtime, and for the first time in weeks, it is a comfortable silence. Maybe it's just my mind that's quieted down, or it's that we've cleared the air and reconnected, but it feels like home again. Whatever this is, I want to keep it forever.

Chapter Fifty-One

KIERA

Things are starting to look up again. It's been a week since the rage blackout, and since then, we've been a lot more in sync. No more hiding feelings, fears or anxiety. We're talking more and becoming closer than we ever have. I'm happy I chose the "bull in a China shop" approach of coming home and sorting stuff out. Ed needs to see I am not going anywhere and that he is the only one for me.

Ed is attending weekly counselling sessions, which are helping him unlock the feelings and fears he's hidden for decades. I'm working my ass off at work as there's a possibility of a promotion coming up soon, and I really want it. I love my role in marketing because I get to create and design campaigns, but if I get the promotion, I'll have my own team. Yes, technically, it's more work, but I want to prove—probably to myself more than anyone—that I can manage a team, get more clients and really boost our company.

. . .

DURING A CONVERSATION ABOUT OUR FUTURE, ED brings up having kids. Although it's something on my life list, I am surprised he bought it up, especially after the last few months and the emotional roller coaster. However, I can picture us with a few kids in a nice big house near where Jess and Gavin have bought one in the countryside just outside of London. I try to suppress the butterflies within me. Is it this simple? Can I really have the man, the house, the life with kids and all?

I'm sitting on my lunch break, thinking about everything we have talked about and find myself scrolling through a property website—just for fun. I mean, it would be a good idea to get a rough estimate of how much houses cost and all that, right? I have a decent savings pot, but Ed and I haven't talked about money. Would we get a joint account? What if one of us has more to contribute than the other? Would this work out if we ever split up and sold the house? I know Ed's been saving and making investments since he was younger, but even with both of our savings, is it enough to buy a beautiful home in the country?

I stop questioning things when I see a house. It looks like many others on here, but there's something about it. I click on the more info button, and it's beautiful. Sandy brick walls, a white porch around the front door and dollhouse-looking windows. I keep scrolling through the photos and stop at the kitchen. I have to have this house. The kitchen is calling to me. It's a modest space with an island and two ovens. TWO! It also has a coffee bar and plenty of space for a large dining table. It's absolutely gorgeous. I scroll through the rest of the photos and, of course, the floor plans. Two separate rooms for offices, four bedrooms, three bathrooms and a large garden, which is currently a blank canvas. Before I know what I'm doing, I text it over to Ed. He probably thinks I'm insane, but this house is too good not to share. Bonus points for it being only a five-minute walk to Jess.

Before I finish my lunch, my phone pings with a message from Ed.

> Ed: Love it. Shall we view?

> Me: What?

> Ed: Did I stutter?

> Me: Smart ass. Are we ready for a house? And we've not discussed how we will pay for it.

> Ed: Booked a viewing for Saturday. We'll discuss it later x

My head is spinning with all the worries of buying a house. Is it too soon? No, we're secure and want this, but… *Stop, Kiera! It's just a viewing.*

I quickly text it over to Jess, letting her know we will be around the corner this weekend and may pop in for a cuppa. Then I tuck my phone away and crack on with work. If, and this is a big IF, we are buying a house, then I need to work my ass off to earn this promotion so that we are in a better financial position. Pushing thoughts of the house and its associated anxieties aside, I work on a proposal for one of my clients.

Walking in the door of our flat, I hear Ed in his office. He's probably still on a call. I set down my bag and coat and go to make us a cuppa, whilst scouring the fridge for what we can have for dinner tonight. I really need to be more organised with our meal planning. We have food, but my brain won't make a meal out of what we have. I pick up some peppers and chicken and see what we have in the cupboards. Deciding on a chicken pesto pasta, I begin prepping dinner when Ed curls his arm around my waist and kisses my neck.

"Hey, you." I smile as I finish chopping and move to the side to wash my hands.

"How was your day?" Ed leans against the island with his muscular arms crossed, making them bulge even more.

"It was alright. I finished my proposal and sent it over to my client. Obviously, there was some browsing going on at lunchtime. How was yours?" I want to gauge his reaction now that we're face-to-face.

"Yeah, it was good. There's a position coming up for Assistant Director of Analytics, and I want to go for it. Looks like we both may be in the running for a promotion soon."

"Oh my God, Ed. That's brilliant news. Do you know who else is in the running for it?"

"Just me at the moment. There are a few other people who have put their hats in the ring, but I'm currently the front runner, according to my boss."

Overjoyed, I launch myself at him to give him a huge-ass hug. We could both be in positions we want soon, and life is finally settling where it should. I finish dinner, and we sit to discuss the house I sent over and are apparently viewing on Saturday, alongside the serious side of funding it. I pour us each a glass of wine as we sit, eat and discuss grown-up shit.

Chapter Fifty-Two

ED

Kiera and I talk through the house. Although it's something I assumed we'd do in our future, planning this with her now makes me happy, and buying a four-bedroom would certainly future-proof us earlier than planned and would also save us from having to move in a few years. I've already spoken to the estate agents and know the owners will accept below the asking price. They've not had many viewings. Therefore, if we do want this house, there's a good chance we'll get it.

We sit and talk through our financials after dinner to work it out together. Turns out, combined, we have rather a lot in savings, and that's not taking into account the stocks and shares I have, which are currently worth around seven-fifty. We decide to keep those where they are to build interest, and we'll cash them in when needed. Kiera is a little shell-shocked when it comes to that revelation, but what can I say? I had nothing to spend it on, so I invested.

We opened a joint bank account after our chat with a savings account attached to it. Once our cards come through, we can activate our account fully and start putting our savings into it. We both get a little excited at the prospect of this house. It looks spectacular, but the one thing for me is that there's plenty of room for development both on the main house and on the grounds. Again, for future-proofing. We've discussed building little bungalows for our parents if they need them, but all the houses would be spaced out enough to ensure everyone has their own privacy.

With the bigger picture in our minds, we sit and look at the smaller pictures, in particular, the floor plans and how we'll design each room. We haven't viewed the house yet, but it's looking promising. I have a friend at work whose sister is a mortgage advisor, and she'll be working with us to get the best rates. I emailed her our figures this evening so she can get to work on that whilst we sit in dreamland about the house.

"How about this one for a nursery?" I question Kiera. She's been quiet about the kid front, and I want to make sure we're on the same page. I feel her shift beside me and turn to face her.

"Ed, do you really want kids? Or is it something you think we should do?"

Shit, we're not on the same page. "I honestly hadn't thought about it until I met you, but when I think about our future, I see us with a few kids around in a kick-ass garden where I can pretend to know how to build playhouses and swing sets." I laugh. It's honestly a daydream I've had. Mainly, it was me swearing at a set of instructions and wooden beams, but it still makes me happy to think about.

Kiera looks deep into my eyes, and I offer no barriers so she can see what I'm saying is true. Eventually, she seems satisfied and grins. "I want two or three big-ass playthings in the garden, a playroom, and I want to learn how to bake, so I don't feel like shit for buying cakes for school, especially when I can imagine the parents in the area we want to move to always bake with their expensive gadgets."

I offer her my most genuine smile. The thought of Kiera growing our baby inside of her fills me with excitement. An image of our future flashes through my mind. I can see us with a few kids and being pretty awesome parents. First, though, I need to wife her up. My mind sets to work on a plan as we chat and then head to bed.

I saw the ring I wanted to buy her months ago. It's small and elegant, with white diamonds surrounding a black sapphire. Kiera isn't one for a large statement ring, so I'm hoping she'll love my choice. We lie in bed, cuddling as we drift off. I feel light and happy, and sleep finds me easily tonight.

IT'S SATURDAY, AND WE HEAD DOWN TO SEE THE HOUSE. Kiera is as excited as a kid at Christmas, and I'll be honest, I'm feeling a little excited, which is amazing considering that not long ago, I couldn't feel many emotions other than anger. I've been keeping my appointments with Dr Gordon, and we've made real progress, which has been enlightening. I feel like a huge weight has been lifted.

Pulling up the drive of the house, the tyres of the car crunch on the gravel driveway. There's a young man, I'd say early twenties, standing by the front door with a big salesman smile plastered on his face as we open our car doors.

"Hi there. You must be Ed and Kiera. I'm Tim." He holds out his hand to me and then Kiera. We both say our hellos as he talks about the front of the property and the grounds. As we enter through the dark, wooden front door, I'm hit with a feeling that I'm meant to be here. Glancing around at the entrance hall, I can see a few things I'd modernise, and I've already mapped out where I'd put the security cameras. You can't have a house this big without security.

Kiera is bouncing as she walks, her head spinning left, right, up and down, taking in every inch of the house as we tour it. We enter one of the rooms we would allocate as an office, and Kiera is talking about floor-to-ceiling bookshelves and putting her desk over by the window that overlooks the back garden. The fact we're both picturing our lives here is a great sign.

We wander around, taking in the character of the house. I checked out a few of the other aspects, such as the main bathroom, which can do with some re-grouting, but otherwise, the house seems in great condition.

I could definitely see us living here and making it ours. Tim has finished showing us around, and we're free to go back around ourselves, which is nice. We can go through room by room, pausing to see where our furniture would sit and what other ideas pop into our heads.

Chapter Fifty-Three

KIERA

I call Jess the minute we leave the house, and we go around to theirs, which is also lovely. I hadn't seen her in ages, and we talked for a long time and ended up staying for dinner. Naturally, we discuss anything and everything. We spend a good twenty minutes talking about wood and then another half hour talking about "wood" when the boys are out of earshot.

After sleeping on it and then putting the offer in on the house, it is accepted within an hour. We instruct our solicitors and are currently filling out a million pieces of paperwork. I swear you have to sign over the rights to your firstborn when buying a house. We send over the initial paperwork, which is, thankfully, all electronic—I would hate to think how many trees would have suffered for this. I have no doubt we'll have to fill out thousands of other forms.

I didn't realise how exhausting paperwork could be. After we've signed our life away, we flop down on the sofa and nibble on oven snacks as neither of us can be bothered to cook, and who doesn't love random oven food for dinner?

It'll take some time for the solicitors to go through our paperwork and everything in between, so we start looking at things we want for the house. We feel quite confident this will go through with no issues. I've gone into full-on project manager mode. One wall of our office in the flat has a giant floor plan of the house with lots of sticky notes attached to it with where furniture can go, what we want the rooms to look like, and what other bits we want to go in the house. We're not ordering anything until we have the email to say the purchase has gone through, just in case, but we are getting prepared.

I sit on the sofa with my phone in hand, scrolling through Pinterest. I feel like I've fallen down a rabbit hole. I began by looking at panelling, and now, I'm viewing pictures on how to build a media wall. I have to stop scrolling, but I can't. What if I miss something worth saving? Social media sucks.

Half an hour flashes by, and Ed grabs my phone out of my hand. "Enough Pinterest for one night, love."

I laugh, thankful the pull of more wall designs has been stopped, and head over to the bathroom to get ready for bed. When I get into bed, my eyes close, and I'm still thinking of different designs for each room. I put on some soundscapes to shut down my mind and drift off into a deep sleep.

"This needed to be done last week, Sarah. I know we've all been busy, but how has this been missed?" I run my hand over my face. We're hours away from a deadline, and a large piece of work has been missed by someone else on my team. Just what I need for a Friday lunchtime. "Right, this is what we're going to do…" I rattle off a list of instructions and get a couple of other team members in on it. Within the hour, the work is done, and I'm reviewing the final piece before sending it over to the client. As exasperated as I was, we've all pulled it together in time. I email it over after I give it a "I'm happy that it's good enough."

Five rolls around, and I pack up my desk, but as I zip up my laptop bag, my manager pops her head round the corner. "Kiera, you got a minute before you leave?" Oh, those words will never cease to fill my stomach with rocks.

"Yeah, no worries." Mandy is a good manager. She generally leaves me to it as I crack on, and I never fail to meet my deadlines. I walk into her office and sit down, my fingers entwining with each other to stop me from fiddling.

"Kiera, I wanted to talk to you before the news went out on Monday. A decision has been made about the Team Supervisor role you were up for." Those rocks are getting heavier in my stomach. She wouldn't bring me in here unless it was to tell me I didn't get it, which gives me the weekend to prepare my "Oh well, maybe next time" face. I simply nod and will her to continue.

"You've worked your ass off, especially with what I saw this afternoon. We have every faith that you'll make a great leader and thrive for yourself and the company. The job is yours."

Did I hear her correctly?

"It's mine? I got the promotion?" I try to keep my emotions in check, but I can feel the excitement thrumming through me like an electric current.

"Yes, you deserve it. Now, go home and celebrate with that gorgeous man of yours." Mandy grins and closes her laptop.

"Oh my GOD!!! Thank you so much. I won't let you down." I shake her hand, which seems way too formal for our conversation, but I need to do something with this energy. I'm positively buzzing. Grabbing my bag, I leap out of the office and call Ed. He must already be on the tube as his phone goes straight to voicemail. Deciding not to leave a voicemail, I power walk to the station and high tail it home.

I rush through the door, and it's dark. Ed's not home. Strange, but I put my stuff away and see what we've got in the kitchen for me to make for dinner. As I close the fridge, the front door opens, and Ed enters with something that has my nose leading the rest of my body to him.

"Mmm. What did you bring home?"

"Thought we could have tapas tonight. We've had a long week, and I can't be arsed to cook. So tapas."

"I couldn't love you more." I grab the bag and take

it to the island as he removes his coat and puts his bag in the office. I finish plating up and take our food over to the sofa. My mouth is watering. I head back and grab a bottle of wine and our glasses before sitting down and filling my mouth with delicious Spanish flavours, honey chorizo, spiced pork belly and garlic mushrooms, just to start. I suddenly feel like I could eat a horse.

Halfway through shoving food into my face, I remember I haven't told Ed my big news. I slap his arm whilst I'm hurriedly chewing, which causes him to jump and pat my back. I finally swallow my food and take a breath.

"My God! I thought you were choking!"

"Haha! I wasn't. I wanted to tell you I got the promotion! I forgot to tell you when you walked in. I was too distracted by food."

"Kiera, that's amazing news! Congratulations. I'm pleased I got us takeout for dinner, but we will celebrate properly over the weekend." Ed beams at me and gives me a sweet kiss that tastes like honey and garlic.

Chapter Fifty-Four

ED

It's been five weeks since we signed form after form for the house, and in that time, we've heard nothing. I'd be concerned, but after speaking to friends at work who have bought houses, they said it could take months. So we sit and wait. I want to start organising, but without a completion date, it has gone on the back burner. Instead, I focus my energy on how I'm going to propose to Kiera. I bought the ring weeks ago and have booked us a table at Marco's restaurant for tomorrow night. It's not out of the ordinary for us to eat out on a Friday, so it shouldn't be suspicious.

I've been keeping the ring in my wallet in a velvet pouch to ensure she doesn't find it—can't have her stumbling on the surprise. I did the gentlemanly thing and spoke to her dad first. He, of course, was delighted, and I could hear her mum screaming in the background. I'm hoping they can keep shtum and not let on that they know. My parents are fully aware of

my plan and are incredibly supportive. They love
Kiera, and Mum has already mentioned grandbabies.

I'm working from home today. Kiera is on the
other side of our office, which is in an absolute state, so
she's having a great day. She started her new role a
couple of weeks ago and is thriving. She's really
enjoying managing the team and multiple projects—a
natural leader, that one. I, on the other hand, am still
waiting to hear about the promotion at work. Apparently, we should be hearing by the end of the week.

I get up to make us some lunch when Kiera wheels
her way over to where I'm standing with a mischievous
look in her eyes. "What you doin'?" she says, snaking
her hands around my waist and grabbing my ass,
pulling me closer. My crotch is now in direct line with
her mouth. Oh, my mind is racing.

"Going to make us some lunch. What are you
doing, Missy?" I cock my head at her with a smile.

Kiera's hands slide from my ass down to my thighs
and round the front. With her hands planted on my
legs, her thumbs are circling dangerously close to my
cock, which is hardening. Her eyes are glued to mine as
she painstakingly slowly makes her way to my belt.

"I know what I want for lunch." Licking her lips,
she undoes my belt and jeans, sliding them down
enough to release my cock from my boxers.

I can do nothing but groan when her lips delicately
touch the head of my cock. My God, her simple touch
is amazing. Kiera's lips part, and her tongue laps up
the beading precum as my hands tangle in her hair.
Taking her time, she licks my shaft up and down before

wrapping those sweet lips around my cock and sucking. Gathering her hair in one hand, I let her build her pace. Her ocean blues are staring up at me with fire in them. Bracing her hands on my thighs to steady herself, she sucks me as if her life depends on it, and my grip on her hair gets tighter as I guide her, so she takes me deeper.

Fuck me, I am about to blow. I grab her head with both hands and pump myself into her beautiful mouth. Tears are threatening to fall from her eyes, but her throat is relaxed as she takes me balls deep. Kiera's grip tightens around my thighs as I pump faster and deeper, coming hard straight down her throat. When I finally still, she uses that delectable tongue to clean my cock and wipes the drool from the corners of her mouth. Fucking beautiful.

Leaning down, I kiss her hard and can smell her arousal from here. We can't have my future wife feeling needy, now, can we? I kneel down and push up the skirt of her dress. Her thighs are glistening with her arousal. Like a starving man, I push her to lean back in her chair and pull her knees further apart, wasting no time to slide her underwear to one side. I dive in with my tongue. Kiera releases a carnal moan as she rests the heels of her feet on her chair, spreading her knees wider. I circle my tongue around her clit whilst pulling her underwear down into the crease of her cheeks, creating pressure on her tight little ass, and she grabs my hair. Pushing two fingers inside her, I increase the pressure with my tongue. Within minutes, Kiera is coming all over my face, and I'm lapping her up.

As she comes down from her high, I lean in and kiss her thigh. "Feeling better, gorgeous?"

"God, yes. Now I'm ready for lunch."

I laugh and make my way into the kitchen, doing my jeans as I go. Kiera hops into the bathroom to tidy up as I make us toasties for lunch. I'm going to enjoy being with her for the rest of our lives.

Chapter Fifty-Five

KIERA

H air, check. Makeup, check. Outfit…well, my wardrobe is currently thrown around our bedroom as I stand in my lacy black thong and matching bra. We're going out to Marco's tonight, that gorgeous little Italian Ed introduced me to when we first met. I'd normally throw on anything, but my spidey senses are telling me to make an effort tonight.

I shave to within an inch of my life, moisturise to high heaven, and make an effort with my hair and makeup, but not too much that I look like I'm going out on the town. With my hands on my hips, I stare at the mess I've created when Ed walks in and laughs.

"What happened? All your clothes begging to be worn at once?"

"Oh, shut up. I don't know what I want to wear tonight."

"That beautiful peach number you have. It's always been my favourite."

I smile, remembering him giving me advice when I went on that one date. Decision made. I put the rest of my clothes away and slide into my peach dress. It hugs my figure perfectly. When I'm ready, we head down to the station and get the tube into town. The train is quiet for a Friday night, so we get seats. I enjoy people-watching on the train. There's an old couple a few seats down the carriage from where we are. They look like they're dressed in their Sunday best as they hold hands and talk to each other. I grab Ed's hand, thinking *I hope we're like that when we reach their age.*

My thoughts are disrupted when Ed pulls me up from my seat. I didn't notice we'd arrived at our stop. We stroll through the streets of London, talking about everything and nothing at the same time. Dusk is settling in the night sky, turning it a beautiful pink colour. It's a wonderful night, and I cannot wait for Marco's cooking. I'm going to try his special tonight, whatever that might be.

We sit down at our table, and Ed orders us a bottle of wine and talks to Marco in Italian. Marco's smile is so wide there are crinkles in the corners of his eyes, which have a glint of excitement in them. This makes me suspicious. What are these two up to? Maria comes over with our bottle and greets us warmly with a kiss on the cheek. She pulls Marco away to the kitchen, and Ed pours our wine.

"What were you two talking about?" I ask, leaning back in my chair and sipping the beautifully crisp white wine.

"Oh, just catching up," Ed responds, but he sounds

odd. If I was a mistrustful person, I might be worried, but I'm not concerned. I know he's been waiting to hear about his promotion, the decision of which should have come out today.

"Any news on the promotion?" I flip through the menu, already knowing I'm having the special, but I want to look anyway.

"Oh, I haven't checked my emails in a while." He puts down his menu and scrolls through his phone.

Maria comes by our table, and we order, both having the special of the night and a couple of sides to share. When Maria totters away, I see Ed frowning at his phone.

"What's up?" I reach over to place my hand on his. I hope it isn't bad news.

"I didn't get the promotion I was going for. Assistant Director would have made a great title…"

"Oh Ed, I'm—"

"They offered me Director of Analytics." His voice is quiet, almost like he doesn't believe what he's reading.

My hand tightens around his, and my excitement for him is bubbling to the surface. "Ed, that's amazing news! Wow! What do you think?"

He finally glances up from his phone, frown lines prominent, but a smile is working its way onto his face. "I…I don't know. I wasn't expecting this at all. I didn't know this was an available position. Do you mind?" Ed points to the door, indicating he's going to make a call.

"Go!" I say a little too loudly. Ed jumps up and rushes out of the door with his phone to his ear.

I sit and drink my wine and watch Ed as he paces back and forth in front of the restaurant. His facial expression turns from a frown into a wide grin and back to a frown. It's like watching a silent movie, except there's no subtitles. When Ed finally comes back to the table, he takes a rather large gulp of wine and a deep breath. I wait patiently to hear the outcome of the conversation.

"So, turns out our director had a health scare, and he has re-prioritised his life. He wants to spend more time with his kids and at home, so that's what he's doing. They want me to take over and learn from him for the next three months whilst he's carrying out his notice period. He's absolutely fine health-wise, but yeah, I'm going to be the next Director of Analytics if I want it." He takes another breath, and I place my hand in his.

"Do you want it?"

His eyes sparkle, and I already know the answer. Ed is ambitious and will be a great leader. This was his end game, so to get here early is fantastic. "Absolutely. I accepted on the spot and start in two weeks when the director is back from holiday."

I leap up, causing my chair to scuffle along the floor. Other patrons turn to stare, but my focus is on grabbing Ed's face and kissing him with everything I have. "Congratulations, babe. I'm so proud of you." The grin is nearly splitting my face in two, but at this moment, I couldn't be happier if I tried.

Maria chuckles and alerts us to her presence. She's carrying our dishes and places them in front of us. "Ed got an amazing promotion. How awesome is that?" I say with pride in my voice. She grins and congratulates him with a warm embrace.

"Only one more thing, and you'll have everything, dear friend." She winks and returns to the kitchen.

I stare after her for a second, trying to piece together what she said. Everything? When my attention lands back on Ed, he's in front of me on one knee. My hands fly to my face as tears well in my eyes, and I gasp. Am I going to look foolish if he's just tying his shoe? Probably. Do I care? Not in the slightest.

Chapter Fifty-Six

KIERA

Ed is staring up at me and takes my hand. In my periphery, I notice Maria and Marco standing nearby, and the other patrons have quieted down. I can't breathe.

"Kiera, I knew from those first few weeks that you were the one I wanted to spend the rest of my life with. You're the light to my darkness, my other half. I promise to always be your partner in everything. Will you do me the honour of becoming my wife?"

Tears fall down my face, and my cheeks ache because of my wide grin. My heart is banging in my chest, and I know there's only one answer I'll ever give to this man. "Yes! Yes, I'll marry you."

Ed grabs my left hand and slides the most beautiful ring I've ever seen onto my finger. He kisses me like no one is watching, but in reality, the whole restaurant is watching, cheering and clapping. I can hear Maria sniffing as she walks over to us.

Ed whispers in my ear, "I fucking love you." Before he stands and is embraced by the giant that is Marco, Maria pulls me up off my chair, looks at the ring and hugs me.

We're engaged!

As we settle back down to eat our dinner, I take a picture of my ring and send it to Mum and Jess before shovelling food into my mouth. I'm absolutely starving, but my stomach took a gracious silence during the last ten minutes. Maria pours us champagne, and Ed and I can't stop smiling whilst eating. Marco and Maria insist that dinner is on the house to celebrate Ed's promotion and our engagement.

When we are done, we walk out hand in hand, grinning like the cats that got the cream, but once outside, I jerk Ed to a stop. "I fucking love you, too," I say breathlessly as I kiss him, one that I don't want to stop, but I also want to get home and ride him hard. Laughing at my internal thoughts, we race to the station to get home.

In the last two months, both Ed and I have climbed the career ladder and got engaged, and we finally have progress on the house, which we'll be closing on tomorrow. It's a lot of excitement, stress and happiness, which, let's face it, is definitely overdue. We've been packing up the apartment and have arranged movers for next week. Decorators are going in the day after tomorrow to start the work, which they promised will be done by the time we move. Luckily, there's nothing major to be done, so a lick of paint and some re-grouting shouldn't take long at all. It's all systems go.

I glance around the apartment at the piles of boxes. It doesn't feel that long ago that I was unpacking my boxes when I moved into Ed's. Now, we're packing up and moving into a house. It feels surreal. I've been a grown-up for a long time, but buying a house seems to be the most adult thing you can do.

With ninety per cent of our stuff packed, we're living out of one suitcase for the next week and mainly living off of simple meals and takeaways. We're currently sitting on the sofa, waiting for our Mexican to arrive, and Ed is scrolling through something on his phone. Although my hands are doing the same, my thoughts are wandering. So much has happened in the last year. Now, buying a house is quite dramatic in and of itself with all the reports, surveys and boring paper-work, but it's the most chilled we've been in a long time. It's nice. I allow my brain to drift whilst staring at my phone.

I made a list a while ago about what I wanted my future to look like. What is on it again?

- Easy and comfortable relationship – check.
- Someone who loves me unconditionally – check.
- Pasion – check.
- Love and lust – check.

- Spontaneity – check.
- Reliability – check.
- House with a garden – check.
- Kids.
- Growing old together, but happily, not going through the motions.

Two more things to go. That's quite an achievement, considering when I make a to-do list for cleaning the house, I barely get three things done before I get bored. Looking back, I'm proud of what I've accomplished, but not all of it has been on my own. Ed is someone I literally bumped into and am going to be spending the rest of my life with. We've gone through quite a bit in our first year together, and now, we're moving on to our next chapter.

Our Mexican arrives, and we sit and eat, talking about the plans for moving and the furniture we've ordered. Naturally, I have a timeline of when things are arriving, so it's not overwhelming when we move in. Moving and having new stuff turn up on the same day will be exhausting, but we're going to take some stuff over before we officially move to be prepared, and then we can work around the decorators.

As I stuff pulled pork enchiladas into my mouth, Ed looks at me with a lopsided grin. "Have I ever told you how gorgeous you are when you eat?"

Now I know that's a lie since I can feel food on my

chin. I smack his arm and carry on with my dinner. I bloody love him.

With dinner finished, we tidy up and glance around our apartment. Tomorrow is the day we get the keys to our new house, and although I'm utterly exhausted, I know it is going to be hard to sleep tonight. Luckily, I know a way that will send me off to sleep. I grab Ed's hand and lead him to the bedroom, my body already thrumming with excitement.

Chapter Fifty-Seven

ED

We're standing in our new kitchen. The decorators have done an amazing job of turning this house into the image we had in our minds. Skimming my hand over the marble worktop that I fell in love with as soon as I saw it when we toured the house, I note the moving team won't be here for another forty minutes. That's forty minutes I can definitely put to good use. Kiera is leaning against the back door that overlooks the garden with a coffee in her hand. I come up behind her and wrap my arms around her waist.

"I can't believe we bought a house. Look at all this space." She gestures to the garden, and I know she's talking about the size of our house, too. Moving from a two-bedroom apartment to a four-bedroom house with an office for each of us is quite a change.

"It's ours for eternity, my love." My voice is breathy as I kiss the crook of her neck. Her head falls back on my shoulder as my hands slide across her abdomen, one thumb hooking in the top of her jeans.

"Ed, what are you doing? The movers will be here any minute." I can feel her body tensing.

"They shouldn't be here for about another thirty minutes, according to the ETA they sent through. That's plenty of time for you to come on my face and cock. What a way to christen our new kitchen, eh?" I chuckle as I remove the cup from her hand and place it in the sink.

I turn her around to face me and grin as I lean in to kiss her. I love how her breath hitches like it's our first kiss. Deepening the kiss, I grab her ass and lift her up. Kiera's legs wrap around my waist as I take her over to the countertop and have her lay back a little so she's propped on her elbows.

Making quick work of dragging her jeans down to her ankles, I push her knickers to one side before I dive between her legs. There's no time for courting today. I need to make her come fast and hard. Hearing her pant as I circle her clit with my tongue spurs me on. I push a finger into her, and a guttural moan rumbles through her. I can feel her body responding as I increase the pressure with my tongue and add another finger. My cock is hardening against my jeans, and I can't wait to get inside her. Swirling my tongue and curling my fingers to find that delicious spot, I push and feel her contract around my fingers and drench my tongue. She shouts my name, and it echoes off the kitchen walls.

Giving Kiera seconds to recover as I shove my

jeans and boxers down to my knees, I line up and sink inside of her. "Fuck, Ed!!" she screams as I drive into her, feeling her slick pussy clenching around my cock as I push her through another orgasm. Wrapping one arm around her back, I pull her up to face me so I can kiss her as I pump into her, chasing my own orgasm. I feel my cock swelling as Kiera digs her nails into my shoulders, coming again and making me crash over the edge with her. Breathless, we stay there for a minute, basking in the afterglow.

I'M COMING OUT OF WHAT FEELS LIKE A DEEP SLEEP. My ears struggle to hear the traffic over the combine harvester that sleeps next to me. The bed feels the same, but I can't hear my usual wake-up sounds. I open my eyes as my brain finally catches up. We live in the country now, and I must have slept like a log after unpacking yesterday. Who knew moving would be so exhausting? I turn over to check the time on my phone. It's just after eight in the morning. We have a lot to do today if we want to stick to our plan. I roll over and plant a kiss on Kiera's cheek, and she doesn't even twitch. Honestly, this woman sleeps like the dead.

I get out of bed, leaving Kiera for a little longer whilst I pad downstairs to make us a coffee. The first rule of moving is to set the bed and coffee machine up first, and everything else will fall into place. Going back upstairs with our coffees, I find Kiera sitting up in bed, grinning at me as I walk over to her.

"Good morning, handsome." She takes her coffee, those blue eyes still waking up.

"Good morning, beautiful." I slide back into bed and sip the hot drink as we plan out our day. First things first is building the new furniture so we can get stuff put away properly. We finish our coffees, throw on some clothes and crack on.

Lunchtime has rolled around quickly as we take a break. We've built all of the new furniture and managed to organise some more of the boxes. We're going to need a skip to take away all of the rubbish. We have a food shop being delivered today to save us some time, but for now, it's the pre-packaged sand-wiches I bought yesterday for our lunch. Wolfing those down with a drink, we move on to the next task, which is a mammoth one. Unpacking Kiera's clothes is going to take a good few hours.

"My God, Kiera. Have your clothes been breeding since we packed them?" I huff as I lug another box into our room to unpack. This is box seven. We put built-in wardrobes into our room so we had more space, and I swear to God, this isn't going to be enough.

"Stop complaining. There can't be that many more left."

I go into the spare room and find three more boxes marked Kiera's clothes, along with five of mine. I bring two more boxes in and begin to separate some wardrobe space for my clothes. She could do a sale like the character Rebecca did in *Confessions of a Shopaholic* and make thousands.

Four hours after we started unpacking clothes, we finally finished in time for the shop to arrive and be put away. As Kiera puts away the rest of the groceries, I make us a coffee and clock the time. I'm not particularly hungry, but thankfully, we ordered some picky bits for dinner so we could snack and unpack at the same time.

"Right." Kiera stands with one hand on her hip, checking the schedule on her phone.

"We have two more things to check off for today, and then we can chill. Our offices." She stands, grinning. Her passion for projects knows no bounds. We drink our coffees and head to our respective offices. We built the desks yesterday, so all we need to do is unpack. I stand in my office and enjoy the calm space. I have a window overlooking the garden, and my walls have been painted sage green. The shelves the decorators put up match the wood tones of my desk, and I cannot wait to get organised. I start with my IT set-up and go from there.

An hour later, I check in on Kiera, whose office has been painted peach and has floor-to-ceiling bookshelves. She also has a window overlooking the garden and is, of course, sitting in the middle of the floor, surrounded by piles of books.

"Let me guess, you want them organised a certain way?" I raise an eyebrow at her.

She smiles and simply says, "Who wouldn't?"

Chapter Fifty-Eight

KIERA

A month ago, we moved into our dream home. It took us four days to set up and unpack, but since then, we've been moving bits around to how we want them. It's a beautiful day, and I sit in the garden with an iced coffee and a book waiting for Ed to finish a call. It's not been long, but I already feel our stress decreasing from living out of the city and being surrounded by fresh air. I've been able to see Jess a bit more, which is wonderful, especially since she's helping plan the wedding and is naturally my matron of honour. Gavin will be Ed's best man. Having our wedding and honeymoon rolled into one sounds lovely. Besides, who doesn't love a beach wedding?

I've already found a dress online. As much as I enjoy shopping, the idea of traipsing around shop after shop for an expensive dress exhausts me, and although my mum was disappointed not to get the dress shopping experience, I said we could go out for her outfit.

The dress I've found is simple, elegant, and not at all what I pictured myself wearing for a wedding dress, but I couldn't resist. It's an ivory trumpet-shaped gown that hugs all my curves and flows out at the bottom. It has no train, but it does have simple straps and sparkles along the hem. It's being delivered next week, so I can try it on. With a wedding abroad, we decided to get married later this year, an autumn wedding in the sun. So, with four months to go until we leave for Morocco, everything is in place, and the paperwork has been filed.

Ed strolls out into the garden, and I notice that his hair is getting long. He's complaining about needing a haircut, but I love that it's falling past his ears. It gives him a bad-boy edge that I'm all over. I put my book down as he leans in to kiss me.

"All finished for the day?" I ask as he stands, his hands sliding into his pockets.

"Yep, and ready to get wedding planning." His smile reaches his eyes as he holds out his hand for mine.

We sit in my office, which is half library, some office and is now also wedding planning central. We have a lovely small circle of friends and family who are coming out with us. We're going to spend a week in Morocco before we get married and then have a two-week honeymoon. The others will join us for the first week, which will be special.

With mine and Ed's outfits sorted, I gave Jess free rein on what she wears as my matron of honour, and as Ed's best man, Gavin shouldn't be hard to dress.

The man lives in suits. The mothers are dizzying about what they want to wear. Whereas the dads want to wear chino shorts and a nice shirt, which we have no issues with, but the mothers want them smart.

The hotel is sorting the flowers, cakes, dress steaming, and pretty much everything else to do with the wedding. Flights are booked, a marriage licence applied for, and we can now sit back and wait for the day. I know weddings are meant to be stressful, but this has honestly been fun to plan. We look at our handiwork for the wedding and grin. Both of our jobs have approved the three weeks off, and I'm already preparing a handover document for my team so they can manage without me for that time.

***

T-minus three days until we leave for Morocco. Jess has emailed me and the hotel the final list of things to do when I get there. Everything is sorted, and it's time to pack. I can practically hear Ed groaning in his thoughts. We bought new luggage for this trip. It is going to be three weeks, and I cannot survive on one suitcase whilst we're there.

"Kiera, we have a weight limit, remember?" Ed laughs as I shove clothes into my second case. My third case is reserved for my dress, shoes and accessories for the big day.

"Yes, dear. Are you sure you've remembered everything in that one suitcase for a THREE-WEEK holiday?" I roll my eyes at him and swiftly receive a smack on the backside as my answer.

"Careful with those eyes, my love." Ed's voice lowers, and my knees weaken a little. Damn him.

Ed grabs and kisses me fiercely before placing me back in front of my suitcase with another smack to the backside. "I'll punish you later for that. Now, finish packing before you stress-pack the entire house." Rolling my eyes and laughing, I finish.

I check my packing list after another half an hour of folding and placing my stuff into suitcases. I'm done, thankfully, but God knows how much these things weigh. I call Ed up to help me down the stairs with them.

"Jesus, Kiera! I was joking when I mentioned packing the entire house. Let me get the scales." Ed weighs our suitcases, and thankfully, each case is still within our weight budget, with a little wiggle room to bring stuff back.

And as promised, I received my punishment, three orgasms and a little nap, all before dinner, which Ed cooked whilst I packed.

Two more days until we fly out to Morocco.

Nine more days till the big day.

When we fly home in just over three weeks, I'll no longer be Miss Kiera Cole. I'll be Mrs Kiera Green.

Chapter Fifty-Nine

ED

We've been in Tamouda Bay, Morocco, for five days, and our wedding is in two. The hotel has been phenomenal, getting everything ready for us. We've seen the beach location where the ceremony will take place, and it's nothing but beautifully picturesque with the golden sand and white canopies.

Kiera has spent a couple of hours a day in the onsite spa with Jess, doing hair and makeup trials, getting massages and facials and doing everything in between. We've all chosen to have the private villas on site. Each has its own pool and beautiful sea views. With what I have planned for the next couple of weeks, I don't want neighbours in the hotel complaining about the noise.

Gavin and I sit at the pool bar, soaking up the sun and talking business. He's a nice guy once you get past the stony wall that he puts up as a first impression.

"So, what's married life like?" Gavin turns to me with his head cocked to one side.

"It's the same as it was before, but Jess knows she's mine, and that's it. Until death do us part, and someone will have to pry her from my cold dead body before I'm ready to leave her."

"Wow. Intense."

He chuckles and lifts his glass to his lips. "It's honestly the same, but the primal need is more intense. She's mine; I'm hers."

I smile, knowing about primal needs. All I can think about is Kiera's body currently being covered in oil.

We switch topics to what he and Jess are going to be doing whilst they're here after the wedding, and honestly, I'm mentally adding a couple of the museums and the quad biking to our own itinerary.

Just as we're about to go for a round of golf—something neither of us can actually play, so it should be a laugh—I spot the girls out of the corner of my eye. Kiera and Jess wave as they disappear into the next building. Nails, if I remember correctly.

We're a half-hour into our round of golf, and I call bullshit on Gavin. There's no way in hell he's not played before, and if he's a natural, then he really is as perfect as Jess keeps saying.

"Oh, come on, man!"

Gavin laughs as he hits the perfect drive. Jammy sod. "Honestly, I've never played before, but I might take it up. We could hit the local driving range to work on your swing." He is laughing again as I swing, and a chunk of grass goes flying as my ball remains perfectly still on the tee. This is going to be a long afternoon.

———————

It's the morning of the wedding, and as per Jess's instructions, she has stayed in our villa with Kiera, and I've stayed in theirs with Gavin. Luckily, the man has great taste in Scotch. I'm fresh out of the shower and sitting on the veranda in my towel with a cup of coffee, taking in the view. I can't wait to see Kiera and wife her up. Although she didn't go to numerous shops for her wedding dress, she never let me have a peek at it, and to prevent temptation, it's been kept at Jess's until we packed for the wedding.

In an hour, I'm going to be a married man. My future awaits.

Gavin and I stand on the decking under a white canopy, our close friends and family sitting on the chairs in the sand, waiting patiently for the music to start. Just as I fix my tie, the piano notes begin to serenade us, and I see Kiera's dad with her on his arm at the end of the walkway. Even from this little distance, I can tell she looks otherworldly.

As Kiera nears, I see her perfectly. Her hair is in a messy bun, her makeup is natural and light, and her dress...damn! I can't wait to get that off of her later. But her beaming smile has me rooted to the spot. The celebrant begins speaking as soon as Kiera is standing next to me. I can hear the blood pumping in my ears.

"We are gathered here today to celebrate the union

of Kiera and Edward…" His words fade as I stare into the eyes that are making the ocean next to us weep with jealousy.

"Edward, do you take Kiera as your wife, your life partner, your equal, for richer, for poorer, in sickness and in health, to love and cherish until death do you part?" For a split second, I hear Gavin's words in my head about having Jess pried from his dead one, and I get it. Kiera is forever mine.

"I do."

"Kiera, do you take Edward as your husband, your life partner, your equal, for richer, for poorer, in sickness and in health, to love and cherish until death do you part?"

"I do."

"I am honoured to announce that you are now husband and wife. Edward, kiss your bride."

And with a cheer from our guests, I kiss her. Not the polite kiss everyone sees at most weddings. It is a kiss that will forever bond us together in this timeline and the next.

"I fucking love you. You'll always be mine," I whisper in her ear.

"I fucking love you, too. And yes, I'll always be yours. Now smile for the camera." She giggles as we grin and wave like the penguins from Madagascar.

We walk down the aisle together and on to our reception of drinking, dancing, and, naturally, ensuring Kiera can eat as much as she likes.

Chapter Sixty

KIERA

I'm panting, out of breath, sweating, and coming down from God knows how many orgasms. I thought the sex on your wedding night was a myth, but Jesus, Ed has been on fire! I manage to muster enough strength to peel myself off the bed and sit up.

"You okay there, wife?" Ed grins but is as equally out of breath and covered in sweat as I am.

"Just in need of a shower and a Zimmer frame to help me get there, husband." His head flies back as he laughs whilst standing up.

"Here, let me help." He picks me up bridal style and carries me to the shower. I flop against him as my body now identifies as a jellyfish.

After a much longer shower than intended, due to my jellified state, we relax on the sun loungers around the pool, staring up at a perfectly clear, starry night. I could stay in this moment forever, and apart from the fact that in the distance I can hear Jess screaming, it's quiet and perfect. Ed hands me another glass of wine, and we lay like this for another ten minutes before heading back into the villa, laughing. Apparently, their session has just started, and they're now in the pool.

TWO WEEKS OF WEDDED BLISS SO FAR. OUR FAMILY AND friends left in stages after our wedding, and we've had nearly the whole two weeks to ourselves. We've visited museums, sunbathed, swam, snorkelled and, at Ed's insistence, went quad biking. I took myself to the spa whilst he went to practice golf. Something about Gavin being a cocky sod and being naturally awesome at it. I laughed, but I can truly see a budding bromance there.

But now, I'm sadly packing my suitcases, wondering how I got it all in them in the first place. I haven't bought that much stuff since being here. I mean, yeah, there's the nice blanket from the market we visited, a rug that is being delivered directly because there's no way I can fit that in the suitcases. Oh, and the artwork we fell in love with. But other than the new clothes, which have fit nicely in Ed's suitcase, there's nothing new, so I'm struggling with the logistics. I hear Ed laughing behind me.

As organised as I am, it takes both of us to repack the suitcases to fit everything in nicely, like a big game of Tetris. Once we're finished, we ring to have them collected to take to the hotel's store room and go to lunch before we leave for our flight in just over an hour. Honestly, these three weeks have been stress-free and nothing short of perfect. We eat lunch, and I pop a couple of snacks into my bag to keep me going until we get to the airport. Can't have me getting hungry now, can we? Although I'm ninety per cent sure Ed's started carrying around protein bars to stop the mood swings from being hangry.

Standing outside the hotel, we're soaking up the last of the African sun as our car pulls up. The driver loads our suitcases into the boot, and we slide into the back seat, where I have a little snooze on our forty minute drive to the airport. It's exhausting being this relaxed.

We land with a bump as the great British weather welcomes us home. Luckily, our car is waiting for us to take us home. Although it's not too late in the evening, I can't wait to get home and comfy. I've enjoyed every moment of the sun, but you can't beat autumn turning to winter in the UK and being all cosied up indoors.

We walk through the door to the lights and heating on, and our post is neatly stacked on the dining table, along with flowers and gifts. Jess popped in before we came home, and I'm so thankful she came by to turn the heat on. The chill is definitely noticeable after being in the mid to late twenties and coming back to eleven degrees.

Going to the kitchen, I make us both a nice cup of coffee and out of the corner of my eye, I spy a note on the counter.

Love birds,
> *There's a lasagne in the fridge. Pop it in the oven for forty*

minutes and eat. House is clean, washing was up to date, and I've arranged for your dress to be picked up in the morning to go to the dry cleaners, so have it ready.

Love you!

Jess xx

Damn, I do love that woman. I immediately turn the oven on to get ready for her lasagne and shout out to Ed, who's disappeared upstairs, probably unpacking and getting a washload ready. Very domesticated. Thankfully, one of us is. When he comes down with all of our washing, he reads the note and gives me a huge kiss.

"We did something wrong when we came in." Ed drags me outside into the now drizzling cold.

"What are you doing?" I laugh, wanting to go back in.

"Taking my wife through the doorway properly." And with that, I'm swung into his arms, proper bridal style, and whisked over the threshold.

"I love you, Mrs Green."

"I love you too, Mr Green. Now, get that lasagne in the oven. I'm starving."

Chapter Sixty-One

KIERA

Although we've been married for five months, I still find it odd seeing Kiera Green on my email signature. I stare down at my left hand at the rings on my finger, reminiscing about our time in Morocco. Magical. I'd love to go back there someday to enjoy the sun, but there are also so many other places I'd also love to visit with Ed, and eventually, I want to take our children travelling around the world, too.

Sitting at my desk in the office, I have a total of seven minutes until my next client meeting, and my stomach is feeling all kinds of strange. Being on contraception, I don't always have periods, but I still get the symptoms; however, they are a lot less severe than before. With everything that has happened over the last year with the trial, Ed's counselling, moving house and the wedding…it suddenly occurs to me that I haven't changed doctors. I look up the local doctors near our house and register online to become a patient. Thankfully, things have moved on from filling out forms and waiting an age to be registered. At the bottom of the form, it gives me a section to add if I need an appointment soon. I tick this and list my symptoms.

With that ticked off my mental list, I dial into the next call and sit back as one of my team takes charge. I was given some opportunities when I was at their level to take the lead in client meetings, and I want all of my team to thrive. I worried that I wouldn't be a great manager, but after doing some training and reading a lot of books, I decided to go with my gut. If I train them and raise them in a way that they can easily take over my job whilst maintaining authority and respect, I've done it right.

As the call comes to an end, the client is happy, and I've already seen a summary of the call in my inbox. Brilliant. As I close up the last remaining tasks for the morning, I receive a phone call.

"Mrs Green?"

"Hi. Yes, that's me."

"Hi. It's the doctor's office. You've requested to be registered and require an appointment. We actually had a cancellation for two this afternoon. Can you make it?"

Checking the time, I can make it if I leave in the next forty minutes.

"Absolutely. Thank you. I'll see you then."

I hang up, send a message to the team to say I'll be out for the afternoon, and pack up my bag to head to the station.

I'm incredibly impressed with this doctor's surgery.

When I check in, I don't even sit down before I'm called into the office. The doctor is a middle-aged woman with a kind smile and a relaxed posture.

"What can I do for you today, Kiera?"

"The last week or so, I've been experiencing period-like symptoms, but also peeing more and feeling a bit sick. I can't remember when I had my last contraception as it's been a bit of a stressful year."

"Okay, let's get you to pee in a cup, and then we'll go through some questions."

There's nothing worse than trying to pee in the tiny cups they give you and then carrying it back to the doctor without spilling it or anyone noticing you're carrying a pot of piss.

The doctor sticks some things in the pot and waits a moment before asking me more questions than the Spanish Inquisition.

"Do you think you could be pregnant?"

"Honestly, I don't think so. I mean, we have a lot of sex, but I'm protected from pregnancy, right?"

"Well, you were due your birth control jab seven months ago. I know you said you've been busy, but that's quite a while."

Shit! Have I really been that poorly organised and distracted? With work, I'm so organised that my coffee is scheduled, but I seem to have been lacking in my personal life lately.

"No, that can't be right." I take out my phone. I normally have a reminder to book my injection, and there it is, right in the middle of all the house and wedding stuff...the reminder. I must have forgotten to book in with the doctors. As I'm checking my phone, the doctor is checking the strip. She turns to face me.

"Kiera, you're pregnant."

Well, shit.

I stare at the doctor as she gives me a leaflet for the local midwife and talks through the next steps, like scans. What the actual? Are we ready? Things have moved quickly, and Ed's finally in a great place mentally. What are we going to do?

Don't panic. I'll speak to the midwife, get a scan and go from there. If we decide it's not for us, then we'll make that decision when we get there. I walk out of the doctor's office and go sit in the local park for some fresh air. I need a minute to think and decide how I'm going to tell Ed. As I'm controlling my spiralling thoughts, my phone pings.

Ed: I love you Mrs Green.

I smile, and all the panic, negative thoughts and worries slip away.

Me: I love you too Mr Green.

Epilogue

ED

I leave work bang on five, wanting to get home and chill. This week has been busy, and being a director is a great opportunity but utterly exhausting at the same time, especially for someone who struggles to delegate. However, I'm learning.

Sitting on a packed train, I think about how lucky I am. Yes, I've been through some shit, but haven't we all to some degree? My counselling is going really well. We're unlocking new levels of my brain every couple of months and working out more of the tension that's been hidden away. I'm in a really good place, and Kiera has agreed to sit in on a couple of the sessions, as Doctor Gordon can explain each new level we unlock better than I can. It's really strengthened our communication and relationship.

We've been married for six months now. Morocco is a favourite memory of mine, although thinking about all the hot, amazing sex we have while I'm on a packed train won't do me any favours. I reshuffle my bag to ensure I'm blocking any view of my semi from the public.

I sit and read one of the latest reports from my assistant on my laptop during the journey, mainly to calm my cock down. Living in the city meant quick commutes; however, I enjoy the train ride home to decompress from the day, especially on a lovely winter day such as this. The air is crisp, the sky is now dark but dry, and although we can't enjoy a glass of wine in the garden, we can enjoy one sitting on the sofa with whatever we have planned for dinner.

The walk from the station is pleasantly cold, but I have a spring in my step. I'm in an amazing place mentally, emotionally and physically. I'm not sure I've ever been here before, but I certainly don't intend on leaving. I see our house in the distance and quicken my pace.

I rush into our country escape. I thought I'd miss the buzz of being in London, but the country air is calming. As I put my bag in the office, I walk past Kiera's office and see her messy desk. You can always tell how productive her day has been by the state of her desk. The messier it is, the more productive it's been.

"Ed, you home?" Kiera calls down.

"I am, love. Be up in a minute." It's been just over two years since we've been together, and I still get a flutter in my stomach whenever I'm about to see Kiera.

As I ascend the stairs, I notice her clothes on the floor. She can be a little messy, but this is a whole new level. As I continue, I notice they're strategically placed. At the top of the stairs, I find her dress, then her tights. Her bra is near the bedroom door, with her lacy black thong hanging on the handle. I'm immediately turned on. Grabbing her thong, I smell her arousal on it. I open the door and walk into the most beautiful site. Kiera is kneeling on the bed, completely naked. She's arranged some restraints around her, not able to put them on herself, and there's a piece of card in front of her. She grins, crinkling the skin at the corners of her eyes. I lean down to kiss her whilst picking up the card. It is shiny, like a photo. I cock my head, not quite understanding what I'm seeing.

Then I see it. Right at the top is *KIERA GREEN*.

I look at Kiera. Tears are filling her eyes, and she fiddles with her hands on her lap.

"We're twelve weeks pregnant," she says, a tear slipping down her cheek.

All manner of questions swirls through me. Will I be a good father? Will I be able to protect them? How will this affect us? Will we still have a great sex life? My emotions are rippling through me, but the one emotion that overwhelms them all is pure happiness.

I place the card down on our console table and turn around whilst undoing my shirt buttons.

"I fucking love you," is all I can say before I pounce on her. This is the woman who changed everything when I bumped into her at that bar, the woman I'm happily married to, and the woman who is carrying our first child. Because if we're having one, we are having a whole bunch.

Acknowledgments

Thank you to my readers and followers. I really appreciate you reading my stories, leaving amazing reviews and wanting more!

Maria, Elli and Tracey, I'll always appreciate you being my sounding board and support.

To my family and friends, without you, I wouldn't be able to be living my dream without your unwavering support. Thank you all so much xx

Other books by Elenor Pountain

Elenor Pountain
A U T H O R

Falling for the CEO (#1 of the Falling Series)

Falling with Kiera (#2 of the Falling Series)

#3 of the Falling Series coming soon…

Follow Elenor's socials:

Printed in Great Britain
by Amazon

39626537R00178